THE 100

REBELLION

KASS MORGAN

HODDER

First published in the United States of America in 2016
by Little, Brown and Company

First published in Great Britain in 2016
by Hodder & Stoughton
An Hachette UK company

1

A CIP catalogue record for this title is available from the British Library

Paperback ISBN 978 1 473 64888 3
eBook ISBN 978 1 473 64889 0

Produced by Alloy Entertainment
1700 Broadway
New York, NY 10019
www.alloyentertainment.com

Printed and bound by CPI Group (UK) Ltd, Croydon, CR0 4YY

Hodder & Stoughton policy is to use papers that are natural,
renewable and recyclable products and made from wood grown in
sustainable forests. The logging and manufacturing processes are expected
to conform to the environmental regulations of the country of origin.

Hodder & Stoughton Ltd
Carmelite House
50 Victoria Embankment
London EC4Y 0DZ

www.hodder.co.uk

For my readers,

Thank you for letting my space delinquents into your hearts. Your support means the galaxy.

'Dark a...
Universe, ...

'Fans of *Th...

'Fantastic tee...
characters'

'An adventurous ...

'It's incomparable t...
and the classic *The F...

'I was practically glued...

'An ingenious double-t...
scenario'

'Both books are riveting. The story is exciting and powerful . . . a
great read for young and old alike. It's pure excitement from page
one to the end'   *Seattle P-I*

'If you haven't t...   ...it!'
...ading

Kass Morgan received a BA from Brown University and a Master's degree from Oxford University. She currently works as an editor and lives in Brooklyn, New York.

Also by Kass Morgan and available from Hodder:

The 100

Day 21

Homecoming

CHAPTER 1

Clarke

Clarke shivered as a gust of wind blew through the clearing, rustling the red and gold leaves that still clung to the trees. "Clarke," someone called faintly. It was a voice she'd imagined countless times since arriving on Earth. She'd heard it in the rushing creek. She'd heard it in the groaning branches. And most of all, she'd heard it in the wind.

But now she didn't have to tell herself that it was impossible. Warmth spread through her chest and Clarke turned to see her mother walking toward her, carrying a basket full of apples from the Earthborns' orchard.

"Have you tried one of these? They're amazing!" Mary Griffin set the basket down on one of the long wooden tables, picked up an apple, and tossed it to Clarke. "Three hundred years of genetic engineering and we never came *close* to growing anything like this back on the Colony."

Clarke smiled and took a bite, glancing around the bustling camp. All around them, Colonists and the Earthborns cheerfully prepared for their first joint celebration. Felix and his boyfriend, Eric, were carrying heavy bowls of vegetables grown in the Earthborns' gardens and prepared in their kitchens. Two Earthborns were showing Antonio how to weave branches into wreaths. And in the distance, Wells was sanding one of the new picnic tables with Molly, who'd recently started training with an Earthborn woodworker.

From the sight of them all now, it was hard to believe how much hardship and heartache they'd all endured over the past few months. Clarke had been one of the original one hundred teenagers who'd been sent to Earth to see whether humans could survive on the radiated planet. But their dropship had crashed, severing contact with the Colony. While the hundred had struggled to survive on Earth, the remaining Colonists realized their life support system had failed and they were running out of time. As oxygen levels dwindled, and panic spread, they fought their way to the dropships, which, unfortunately, could only hold a fraction of them. Clarke and the other members of the hundred had been stunned when several dropships full of Colonists landed on Earth. Less surprising: Vice Chancellor Rhodes engaged in a brutal campaign to seize power from the teens, who had become the de facto leaders of the Colonists on the ground. Among other casualties, it resulted in the death of Sasha Walgrove, Wells's girlfriend and the daughter of the peaceful Earthborns' leader, Max, igniting tension between the groups. But they'd eventually come together to defeat a dangerous enemy—the rogue faction of violent Earthborns who wanted to destroy the Colonists—and now everyone seemed to be doing their best to work together. Rhodes had resigned as Vice Chancellor and he helped form a new Council, comprised of both Colonists and Earthborns.

Today wasn't just the first joint celebration between the groups: It was the first time the new Council would appear together before their newly united people. Clarke's boyfriend, Bellamy, was one of the new Council members, and had even been asked to give a speech.

"It looks like everything is coming together," Clarke's mother said, watching a young Colonist help two Earthborn girls lay the tables with rough tin plates and wooden cutlery. "What should I be doing?"

"You've been doing more than enough. Just try to relax." Clarke took a step back and drank in the familiar sight of her mother's warm smile. Though it had been a month since they'd been reunited, she couldn't stop marveling that her parents hadn't been floated back on the Colony as punishment for treason, as she'd been told. They'd been sent to Earth instead, where they'd faced countless dangers and finally made their way back to her. The two doctors had since established themselves as vital members of the camp, helping rebuild after the attacks by the violent Earthborn faction, working with Dr. Lahiri to heal those who were injured, and, along with Clarke, Wells, and Bellamy, tightening the bonds between the Colonists and their peaceful Earthborn neighbors.

For the first time Clarke could remember, life had begun to feel peaceful, and full of hope. After months of fear and suffering, it finally felt appropriate to celebrate.

Clarke's father strode across the clearing toward the rough-hewn tables, pausing to wave at Jacob, an Earthborn farmer he was friendly with, then turned back to fix Clarke with a huge grin. His left arm was crooked around a bundle of brightly colored corn.

"Jacob says the rain will hold off long enough to get a good view of the moon when it comes up." David Griffin laid the corncobs on the table and thoughtfully scratched his bushy new beard, peering into the sky as if he could already see it. "Apparently, it'll be red along the horizon.

Jacob called it a Hunter's Moon, but it sounds like what our ancestors called a harvest moon."

As a child, Clarke had sometimes grown weary of his endless Earth lectures, but now, after a year in anguished mourning for the parents she believed to be dead, his eager chatter made her heart swell with delight and gratitude.

Yet as he spoke, Clarke's gaze shifted toward the tree line where, in the distance, a familiar, tall figure was striding out of the forest with his bow slung across one shoulder. "You know, I kind of like the sound of Hunter's Moon," Clarke said distractedly, a smile spreading across her face.

Bellamy's pace slowed as he entered the clearing, scanning the camp. Even after everything they'd been through together, knowing that he was looking for her made Clarke's heart flutter. No matter what this wild, dangerous planet threw at them, they'd face it together, survive it together.

As he came closer, she saw the bundle hanging on his back. It was an enormous bird with splayed neon feathers and a long, spindly neck. By the looks of it, it would feed half the group tonight. A surge of pride fizzed through her. Although their camp had grown to more than four hundred people, including a number of the Colony's well-trained guards, Bellamy was still far and away the best hunter.

"Is that a turkey?" Clarke's father asked, nearly knocking over a table in his hurry to get a better look.

"We saw them in the woods," her mother said, appearing at Clarke's side. She raised a hand to shield her eyes from the sun as she watched Bellamy approach. "Northwest of here, last winter. I thought they were peacocks, with those blue feathers. Either way, they were too wily for us to catch one."

"Bellamy can catch anything," Clarke said, then blushed when her mother raised a knowing eyebrow.

Clarke had been a little worried about introducing Bellamy to her parents, unsure how they'd react to anyone other than her upstanding Phoenician ex-boyfriend, Wells. But to her relief, they'd warmed to Bellamy right away. Their own traumas made them sympathetic and even protective of Bellamy when he spent the night in Clarke's family's cabin, plagued by debilitating nightmares that tore him from sleep, rendering him a trembling, sweating mess—dreams about firing squads, blindfolds fused to his face, hearing Clarke's and Octavia's screams rattle his bones. On nights like those, her parents scrambled to mix herbal drafts to help him sleep while Clarke held his hand, neither of them ever uttering a word of caution to Clarke.

Both were waving cheerfully to Bellamy right now, yet Clarke felt her shoulders tensing. There was something off about his step. His face was pale and he kept looking over his shoulder, eyes wild and panicked.

Clarke's father's smile fell as Bellamy drew close. He reached for the bird and Bellamy dropped it into his outstretched arms without so much as a thank-you.

"Clarke," Bellamy said. His breath was ragged, as though he had run here. "I need to talk to you."

Before she could respond, he grabbed her elbow and pulled her past the fire pit to the edge of the ring of newly built cabins. She stumbled slightly on a jutting root and had to catch her balance quickly to keep from being dragged behind him.

"Bellamy, *stop*." Clarke wrenched her arm free.

The glassy look briefly left his eyes. "I'm sorry. Are you okay?" he said, sounding momentarily more like himself.

Clarke nodded. "Yes, fine. What's going on?"

The frantic look returned as he surveyed the camp. "Where's Octavia?"

"She's heading back with the kids right now." Octavia had taken the younger children to play at the creek for the afternoon, to keep them from interfering with the preparations. Clarke pointed to the line of children holding hands while they crossed the clearing to the tables, black-haired Octavia leading the pack. "You see?"

Bellamy relaxed a fraction at the sight of his sister, but then, as his eyes met Clarke's, his face darkened again. "I noticed something strange while I was out hunting."

Clarke bit her lip, stifling a sigh. This wasn't the first time he'd said those words this week. It wasn't even the tenth. But she squeezed his hand and nodded. "Tell me."

He shifted his weight from side to side, a bead of sweat trickling out from underneath his dark, tousled hair. "A week or so ago, I saw a pile of leaves on the deer path, on the way to Mount Weather. It seemed . . . unnatural."

"Unnatural," Clarke repeated, trying her best to remain patient. "A pile of leaves. In the woods, in autumn."

"A *huge* pile of leaves. Four times bigger than any of the others around it. Big enough for someone to hide in." He started pacing, talking more to himself than to Clarke. "I didn't stop to check it out. I should've stopped. Why didn't I stop?"

"Okay . . ." Clarke said slowly. "Let's go back and look at it now."

"It's gone," Bellamy said, running his fingers through his already unruly hair. "I ignored it. And today, it's gone. Like someone was using it for something, but they don't need it anymore."

His expression, a mixture of anxiety and guilt, made her heart ache. She knew what this was about. After the dropships had landed, Vice Chancellor Rhodes had tried to execute Bellamy for crimes he'd supposedly committed back on the ship. Just two months ago, he'd been forced to say an agonizing good-bye to the people he loved before being blindfolded and dragged out to meet a firing squad. He'd looked death straight in the eye, believing he was about to abandon Octavia and destroy Clarke. But his imminent execution had been derailed by the sudden, brutal Earthborn attack. Though Rhodes had pardoned Bellamy, those events had taken their toll on him. The bouts of paranoia that followed weren't surprising, but instead of getting better, Bellamy seemed to be growing worse.

"And then you add this to all the other stuff," he went on, his voice louder, more frenzied. "The wheel ruts by the river. The voices I heard in the trees—"

"We talked about this," Clarke cut him off as she wrapped her arms around his waist. "The wheel ruts could have come from the village; Max's people have wagons. And the voices—"

"I *heard* them." He started to pull away but Clarke wouldn't let him.

"I know you did," she said, tightening her hold.

He slumped, resting his chin on her head.

"I don't want to cause a scene . . ." Bellamy swallowed. The word *again* went unspoken. "But I'm telling you. Something isn't right. I felt it before and I'm feeling it now. We have to warn everyone."

Clarke glanced over her shoulder at all the people

milling about the camp: Lila and Graham walking past with buckets of water, teasing a younger boy struggling with his load; Earthborn kids giggling as they ran from their village with more food for the table; guards chatting as they traded patrol positions.

"We need to warn them before this . . . celebration." He waved his hand dismissively. "Whatever this is."

"The Harvest Feast," Clarke said. She loved the idea of participating in a tradition that went back hundreds of years, before the Cataclysm—the nuclear war that nearly destroyed the Earth and forced the first Colonists into space to save the human race. "Max said it's been celebrated here for generations, and it'll be nice to take a moment to—"

"It's what that splinter group of Earthborns is waiting for," Bellamy interjected, growing louder. "If I were going to attack us, today would be the day. All of us together. Sitting ducks."

A little boy skipped out of his cabin, then, seeing Bellamy, blanched and ducked back inside.

Clarke took Bellamy's hands, held them while they shook, and looked him in the eye. "I trust you," she said. "I trust that you saw what you saw."

He nodded, listening, though he was still breathing heavily.

"But you need to trust me too. You are safe here. We are safe. The truce we struck last month is holding firm. Max says that splinter group of Earthborns moved off south as soon as they lost the fight, and there hasn't been one sighting of them since."

"I know," Bellamy said. "But it's more than that leaf pile. I have this *feeling* on the back of my neck . . ."

"Then we'll replace it with a different feeling." Clarke rose onto her toes and kissed the spot under Bellamy's jaw before trailing around to the back of his neck.

"It's not that simple," he said, though she could feel him finally starting to relax.

She leaned back and smiled up at him. "Come on, today is a *happy* day, Bel. It's your first big event as a member of the Council. Think about your speech. Focus on enjoying all the food you helped provide."

"The Council," he said, closing his eyes and letting out a breath. "Right. I forgot about the damn speech."

"You'll be fine," Clarke said, stretching up again to brush his rough cheek with her lips. "You're good on your feet."

"True." He looped his arms around her waist, grinning as he drew her closer. "I'm good *off* my feet too."

She laughed, thwapping him. "Yes, magnificent. Now come help me get this dinner together before you meet up with the Council. We can celebrate *privately* later."

He walked behind her, his arms still wrapped around her waist, his breath warm against her neck. "Thank you," he murmured.

"For what?" she asked lightly, trying to hide the fact that her heart was a drumbeat of mounting worry.

She might have talked him down today. And yesterday. And the night before.

But she could no longer ignore the fact that Bellamy was getting worse.

CHAPTER *2*

Wells

Wells's back muscles burned as he heaved the last barrel of cider into the cart. After days of preparation for the Harvest Feast, his hands were cracked and raw, his feet swollen and aching. Every inch of him was in pain.

And all he could think was: *more.* More pain. More work. Anything to distract from the dark thoughts that infected his mind like rot. Anything to make him forget.

An Earthborn woman carrying a baby in a sling walked by and smiled at Wells. He nodded politely back, bracing himself as a memory slammed into him like a meteor: Sasha dangling a stalk of wheat for the same baby to play with while the mother hung laundry to dry outside her cabin.

Sasha's black hair swinging forward, green eyes flashing as she teased Wells for being more afraid of babies than of facing Rhodes and his troops in battle.

Wells gritted his teeth and crouched to lift the cart, the painful weight of it obliterating the memory; then he pulled the load down the central village path to the edge of the forest, where the others were milling about with their own cargo.

Red-haired Paul, off duty but still wearing his guard uniform, stood on a boulder, overseeing the Earthborn villagers and Colonists who'd volunteered to bring supplies down to the camp for tonight's feast. "Okay, folks, I've done a thorough patrol of the woods and the coast is clear. But let's keep things moving, just in case." He clapped and pointed down the now well-trodden forest path. "Look alive now, and maintain constant awareness."

Wells watched as a few of the villagers shot Paul bemused looks. Paul was a relatively new arrival, one of the Colonists who'd been on a dropship that had landed off course. His group had made its way to camp just after their bloody battle with a violent faction of Earthborns had ended in a truce.

Wells had vaguely known Paul back on the Colony. Affable and energetic, he'd always struck Wells as more of a dependable, competent soldier than a leader, but things had clearly changed in the past year. Whatever had happened to Paul's band of survivors between their crash landing and their arrival at camp, it had made him their unofficial captain, and he still assumed that air of responsibility.

"Those of you carrying heavy loads, take care not to strain yourself. If you're injured, you'll be an easy target for the enemy."

Wells rolled his eyes. The dangerous Earthborns were long gone. Paul was just frustrated to have missed all the action, and was overcompensating for it now. Wells had no patience for that, not after he'd witnessed the real price of battle.

Paul frowned slightly. "Graham, what are you doing with that knife? You're not hunting today."

"Says who?" Graham said, pulling the long knife from its sheath and twirling it in Paul's direction. For a moment, Wells considered intervening. Although Graham had settled down over the past few months, Wells would never forget the violent gleam in his eyes when he tried to convince the original hundred to kill Octavia for stealing medicine.

But before Wells could act, Graham snorted, resheathing his knife, and sauntered off, nodding at Eric, who was coming from the other direction.

Eric walked up to Wells. "Need help with this?" He motioned toward the cart. "You don't want to *strain yourself and become an easy target for the enemy*," he said drily.

Wells forced a laugh. "Sure, thanks. I'm just going to grab some more firewood and then I'll be right behind you."

He turned and headed for the woodpile behind the far row of cabins, smile dropping away, his jaw heavy with the effort of pretending. Everything about him felt heavy these days, each step weighted with grief. But he kept walking anyway, lifted the ax from its perch, and split logs until he had a sizable pile of wood to carry. He stacked it neatly, ignoring the splinters in his palms, wrapped it all in a back sling, and hoisted it onto his shoulders.

The village had emptied out while he was chopping; they'd all left to join the others to eat and celebrate: the harvest, a fresh start, a bigger community, a newfound peace.

Wells exhaled, his shoulders slumping. The straps of the sling cut through his shirt into his skin as he looked around at the vacant valley. This was good. He'd get to the camp a little late but with plenty of wood for the stoves and the bonfire. He'd stay by the fire and keep it stoked. That would be his job tonight, a perfect excuse to avoid the feast, the speeches, the hundreds of familiar faces, all of them thinking about the people they wished were with them tonight.

Their loved ones back on the Colony . . . all dead because of Wells.

He'd been the one to loosen the airlock back on the ship, dooming the hundreds of people who couldn't find seats on the dropships to a slow, suffocating death—his own father, the Chancellor, included. He'd done it to save Clarke, but still, every time he caught sight of his own reflection, he recoiled from it. Every action he took led to destruction and death. If the other Colonists knew what he'd done, they wouldn't just turn him away from today's Harvest Feast tables—they'd cast him out of their community entirely. And he would deserve it.

He exhaled again, and felt himself wobbling, suddenly weak. He turned to steady the heavy load on his back and saw that one of the cabins had its door ajar.

It was Max's cabin. Sasha's home.

Wells had only known Sasha for a few weeks, but it felt like years of vivid memories had built up during that short time. He'd especially loved being with her in the village. She hadn't just been the Earthborn leader's daughter— she'd been part of the community's life force. She was the one who'd first volunteered to gather intelligence on the hundred, even though the mission put her life in danger.

She was the first to lend a helping hand, offer a sympathetic shoulder, or voice an unpopular opinion on behalf of the less powerful. She was useful, she was valued, she was loved, and now she was gone.

Wells dropped his sling, ignoring the clatter of the firewood, and stumbled like a sleepwalker to the doorway. He hadn't been inside the cabin for nearly a month, avoiding both memories and interactions with the grieving Earthborns for as long as possible. But now there was no one around, and the cabin was drawing him in like a magnet.

His eyes searched the dim interior, taking in a table crammed with scraps of electronics, a small kitchen space, Max's sleeping quarters . . . and there, in the back, Sasha's corner.

Her bed, her quilt, a bundle of dried flowers, a drawing of a bird scratched into the wooden wall. All still there.

"I couldn't bring myself to move any of it," came a deep, gravelly voice behind Wells.

He turned to see Max standing a foot away, peering past him with an inscrutable expression. His beard was neatly trimmed, his best clothes neatly darned, all ready for his official role at tonight's festivities. But right now he didn't look like the leader of the Earthborns and a member of the new, united Council. He looked like a wounded man—a father still in the freshest wave of grief.

"She drew that bird when she was five, you know. I thought it was pretty good for that age. For any age." He let out a little laugh. "Maybe in the old world, she could have been an artist."

"She could have been a lot of things," Wells said softly.

Max nodded, then pressed a hand against the wall of the cabin for balance, as if something inside of him had just cracked.

I shouldn't be here, Wells thought, but before he could make an excuse to leave, Max straightened and walked into the cabin, motioning for Wells to follow.

"I prepared a few words to start the feast, but of course, I left them all the way back here," Max said, riffling through his makeshift desk for a little scrap of paper crammed with scribbled words. "The spots at the table are filling up fast. You might want to get over there."

"It doesn't matter. I'm not even sure I'm going." Wells stared at his boots but felt Max's eyes lingering on him.

"You have as much reason to be at that table as anybody, Wells," the older man said. His voice was quiet but firm as stone. "These people . . . *our* people . . . are together because of you. Alive because of you."

Wells's eyes shot to Sasha's corner. Max glanced over his shoulder at it, following Wells's gaze.

"She'll be there too in a way, you know," Max said, his voice softening slightly. "The Harvest Feast was her favorite holiday." He stepped forward, pressing a hand to Wells's shoulder. "She'd want you to enjoy it."

Wells felt his eyes stinging. He cast them down and nodded. Max squeezed his shoulder and let go.

"I'll be sitting up at the head of the table with the rest of the Council," he said, striding out. "I'll save you a seat beside me. You wouldn't want to miss Bellamy's speech, right?"

Despite himself, Wells smiled at the thought of his brother, the brand-new Councilor, giving a speech to hundreds of people. They'd only recently discovered that they were half brothers, but their relationship was evolving quickly, moving from begrudging mutual respect to true loyalty and affection.

Wells followed Max out of the cabin and shut the door gently behind him, letting his gaze linger on the little bird. It was hard to believe that a child had carved it. The young Sasha had captured the animal in mid-flight, making it appear light and joyful, just like she looked on the rare occasion when she set aside her responsibilities and let herself be free. He'd been privileged, he realized, to see that side of her—to watch her shriek with delight as she plunged into the lake from a far greater height than Wells would ever dare. To see her fierce green eyes mellow with tenderness after a kiss. Wells's carelessness had robbed them of a lifetime of these moments, but it couldn't take away the memories stored deep within his heart.

He might not have the right to celebrate tonight, not after all he'd done, all he had to answer for—but he did have plenty left to be thankful about.

CHAPTER *3*

Glass

Silence wrapped around their bed like an extra blanket. This side of the camp had emptied out as everyone left to help with preparation for the Harvest Feast. But Glass had spent the afternoon here, in their little cabin nestled at the edge of the clearing, distracting Luke and being distracted. This was a rare stolen moment for them. Since Luke had recovered from a near-fatal leg wound, he'd become busier than ever. He left their cabin at dawn and returned long after sunset, generally exhausted and with a slight limp that always made Glass's heart twinge.

Luke tried to perch on an elbow, but Glass held him

down, kissing his shoulder, his bicep, his chest, then letting her mouth trail teasingly lower.

He let out a smiling groan. "I've got to get to my shift."

She kissed his chin, his neck. "Not yet."

"You keep making me late." He traced her spine with his fingertips, his expression uncomplaining.

"They won't mind," Glass said, nestling closer. "You get more done in your shifts than anybody else. You've built half this camp." She tilted her head to the side, surveying him with a proud smile. "My brilliant engineer."

Luke had designed two different models: a small structure with a lofted sleeping space for families, and a longer cabin for groups of people to bunk together, like the camp's orphaned children and the guards. But Glass and Luke's cabin was special. It was set back from the others, and its small windows faced the spot where the sun rose over the clearing at this time of year. There was even a fireplace, and a small kitchen area with a table and chairs. No one had batted an eye about them living together, a welcome change after all the time they'd spent sneaking around back on the ship—first because of the oppressive social hierarchy, then later because Glass had been a fugitive.

"I've overseen *some* of the construction," he corrected. "Everybody's worked incredibly hard. Besides, I'm not on a construction shift. I have guard duty this evening." Luke reached up to run his fingers through the blond hair that hung loose around Glass's face like a veil, then sighed against her neck.

Glass knew that sigh. It meant time was up. She smiled and pushed herself upright, giving him room to scoot out of bed and get dressed.

"Why do you need to go on patrol right in the middle of the Harvest Feast?" she asked, pulling her shirt over her head, her toes searching the floor for the thick woolen tunic she'd discarded there hours ago—a welcome gift from their new Earthborn friends. Even inside the cabin, the air had an icy edge to it, and the sun hadn't even set yet. Their first winter was on its way.

Winter on Earth. Glass felt excitement ripple through her at the thought of log fires and blinding white snow and nights wrapped up warm in Luke's arms.

"Somebody's got to do it. Might as well be me," he said, pulling on his boots. He stretched, groaning slightly as his back cracked. "You won't be lonely, will you?" he asked, coming to sit beside her on the little bed. "You can sit with Clarke and Wells."

Glass bumped him with her shoulder. "I'll be fine." Her tone was light, but the truth was that she'd had a harder time adjusting to life at the camp than he had. As a member of the elite engineer corps back on the ship, Luke had made himself useful right away. Glass was a hard worker and did her best, but she wasn't a natural leader like her childhood friend Wells, and she didn't have a clear expertise like Clarke, whose medical training had already saved countless lives. And while Clarke had shown nothing but patience and kindness toward her, Glass couldn't shake the feeling that her old schoolmate still saw her as the shallow girl whose life had revolved around picking up trinkets at the Exchange and gossiping with her equally small-minded friends.

Glass stood, forcing a smile. "We should get going. I told Clarke I'd help her bring food over to the people in the infirmary, so . . ." She nodded to the door. "Onward."

"Yes, ma'am," Luke said with a playful salute. Glass shoved him out the door, and he laughed, hands up in surrender. She watched him jog a few steps ahead of her.

Dr. Lahiri said Luke's recovery had been miraculously swift, but Glass still couldn't look at his leg without seeing the Earthborn spear embedded in it. She had dragged Luke to safety, down rivers and through forests, arriving back at camp just in time to get him the medicine he needed to heal. Wells had called her "courageous," but she'd been acting out of fear and desperation. After everything they'd been through, everything they'd sacrificed, she couldn't imagine life without Luke.

He glanced back at her, clearly wondering why she was taking so long.

She grinned at him and called out, "Just taking in the view."

He raised his eyebrows. Glass skipped closer, grabbed his arm, and pressed herself against him, matching him stride for stride. As they walked past the cabins into the clearing, they got their first glimpse of the festivities: a circle of long tables decorated with wreaths, braided evergreen garlands, and more food than Glass had seen since landing on Earth.

"On second thought, you're right," Luke said wistfully. "It does seem a little unfair that I have to be on duty right now."

"I'll save you some. I promise. Plus dessert."

"Don't worry about the dessert," Luke said. He tilted his head to brush his lips against the nape of her neck before raising his mouth to whisper in her ear, "There's only one thing I want, and I'm not worried about them running out." His warm breath on her skin made her shiver.

"Careful there, soldier!" Paul walked by, shaking his head with mock scorn. "Engaging in intimate activities while on duty is strictly forbidden. Section 42 of the Gaia Doctrine." Paul let out a loud laugh, winked, and continued on his way.

Glass rolled her eyes, but Luke just smiled. "Paul's all right. He just takes some getting used to."

"You'd say that about anybody," Glass said, squeezing his arm tighter. "You see the best in everyone." It was a quality she admired in Luke, although it sometimes kept him from seeing people's true colors, like his creepy friend and roommate back on the Colony, Carter.

At the edge of the clearing stood the newly built watchtower, where the guards kept their weapons. It was the most fortified building in the camp.

One of the younger guards, Willa, emerged from the tower, yawning. "Do you have the next shift, Luke?" she called, breaking into a slow jog as she made her way toward them. "It's completely dead. No signs of activity. There aren't even weapons to look after."

Luke's brow furrowed slightly. "What do you mean?"

"I guess they moved the weapons out?" Willa shrugged. "I left my rifle on the rack but now it's gone."

"Okay . . ." Luke's step stalled slightly. "Thanks, Willa. I'll find out what's going on."

Glass rose onto her toes to give Luke one more kiss, then stood and watched him head inside the tower. Once he'd disappeared, the smell of roasting meat turned her head back toward the rapidly filling Harvest Feast tables. In the center of the clearing, the new members of the Council were standing together, talking animatedly. Bellamy stood off to the side, glancing nervously over his shoulder every few moments. Farther down, Glass spotted Clarke headed to the infirmary on the far side of the clearing, arms laden with platters.

Glass broke into a jog and quickly caught up to her.

"Can I help?" she asked, reaching out for one of the platters.

Clarke looked up at her, clearly frazzled. "I've got it," she said. "But can you do me a huge favor? Can you run and grab some chamomile from the patch by the pond? Some of our patients need it to sleep, and it takes ages to brew."

"Absolutely," Glass said quickly, eager to be of use. "What does it look like?"

"Small white flowers. Bring as many as you can find, roots included."

"Got it. And where's the pond?"

"About a ten-minute walk east. You head toward the Earthborn village, but turn when you get to that pine tree. Then keep going for a bit and turn left at that cluster of blackberry bushes."

"Sorry, which ones are the pine trees again?"

A flicker of irritation crossed Clarke's harried face. "The ones with the needles instead of leaves."

"Right," Glass said, nodding. "And the blackberry bushes will have—"

"Actually, don't worry about it," Clarke cut in. "I'll go myself."

"No, it's fine. I can do it," Glass said. She was sure Luke had pointed out the blackberry bush to her at some point. "I'll find it."

Clarke sighed. "It's just easier if I do it. But thank you. Maybe next time." She hurried away, leaving Glass standing on her own, cheeks burning as she wondered how long it would take for her to stop feeling like an outsider. Or worse, like a burden.

In the distance, Max raised a hand, and the excited buzz of conversation died down enough for Glass to hear. He welcomed everyone to the feast and explained that while the tradition had evolved over the centuries, it'd always been a holiday for giving thanks. "And so, let us all take a moment to think about our blessings, to feel gratitude for what we see before us now, and for the gifts that enriched our pasts." His voice cracked and he paused, sending a jolt of pain through Glass's chest. She hadn't known Sasha well, but she knew the agony of grief. Every night, just as she was drifting off to sleep, an image crept out of the recesses of her mind: her mother, throwing herself in front of Glass on the dropship to protect her, blood blooming bright on her shirt and spreading and spreading until the light dimmed from her eyes.

Max's voice was suddenly drowned out by applause. So many people were standing up, it was hard to see what was going on, but it looked like he was hugging Wells.

Glass took a breath and began walking toward the gathering. If she couldn't be helpful, she might as well join in the festivities. As she neared the tables, a large pinecone dropped from an overhanging branch and landed at her feet. Without thinking, she kicked it away like she did when playing with the children. It bounced once and landed a few meters away, then burst apart.

The light hit Glass first, a blinding flash that seemed to reduce the entire world to searing brightness.

Then came the wall of air, and the shuddering of the heaving earth. She barely had time to process the thunderclap of sound before it was replaced by a piercing whine in her ears.

Her face was in the dirt. Glass wrenched a gasp, and the air that she tasted was smoky and thick and wrong. She pushed herself upward with a feeble groan, her body trembling.

The camp was on fire. She brushed a hot ember off her cheek seconds before another explosion rocked the far side of the clearing, near where the guard tower was. People were shrieking, running. Glass scrambled to her knees, stretching her arm along the ground to pull up whoever was on the ground beside her . . . and realized a second later that it was just a hand. Attached to nothing else.

She shrieked and recoiled. Vomit rose in her throat, but she swallowed hard and fought to stand, screaming, "Luke! *Luke!*"

She couldn't get her bearings and spun three times before she realized why. The landmark she was searching for, the guard tower, was gone. It was no more than a smoldering mound of wood, the whole area around it scorched.

The building Luke had been in was destroyed.

Glass staggered toward the ruins, numb to the protests of her battered body. The only thing she could feel was panic flooding her veins. She tried to scream, but was unable to produce any sound.

Just when she thought she might collapse from the dizzying whirl of fear and grief, she spotted a familiar shape emerging from the cloud of smoke. *Luke.* He was fine; he hadn't been in the building after all. From across the clearing, their eyes met, and she was sure the relief she saw on his face was mirrored on her own.

But then he looked over her shoulder and his eyes widened in fear. She couldn't hear his words, but she was sure he'd said, "*Run.*"

Glass turned around and got a brief glimpse of a tall

man striding toward her. He had a shaved head and was dressed in strange white clothes.

And then he jammed a needle into her neck.

The world went from red-hot to spotty white and then black. As if from a great distance, Glass felt herself falling into nothing.

CHAPTER 4

Bellamy

As people screamed, fled, and fell all around, two thoughts occurred to him:

This can't be happening.

And . . . *I knew it.*

They'd never be safe on Earth.

Then more pressing thoughts sliced through the fog. *Clarke. Octavia. Wells.* From his position at the Council's table, Bellamy scanned the smoke-filled clearing, but his eyes were burning and he could barely make out anyone's face. "Octavia!" His sister's name tore from his throat, but the sound was lost in the din. "Clarke! Where are you?" He lurched forward. He had to keep moving until he found them.

A bone-shattering sound pierced the roar of frantic screams. *Gunfire.* Even half-crazed with panic and fear, Bellamy registered the strangeness of it. The Earthborns who'd attacked them last time didn't have guns.

"Bellamy! Get down!" A forceful hand wrapped around his wrist, wrenching him to the ground. Felix was crouched under the wooden table alongside five or six other trembling figures. "It's coming from the woods . . . oh my god . . . oh my god." Felix gasped. "Eric is out there. He was bringing supplies from the village. Can you see him?"

The thunder of gunfire paused, leaving Bellamy's ears ringing. Their attackers were reloading.

"Everyone, stay down!" Max's voice bellowed from somewhere nearby. But it was too late. As the smoke began to dissipate, Bellamy saw an Arcadian woman he recognized crawl out from under a table and sprint toward the cabins. There was another spray of gunfire, and she fell backward, blood spurting from her neck.

A moment later, Clarke's mother jumped up and was at the woman's side, pressing her hand against the woman's neck. A new round of bullets tore through the air and she flattened herself against the ground.

"Mary!" Bellamy shouted. "Come back!" But he knew he was wasting his breath. Whatever gene kept most people from risking their lives to save others, the Griffin women didn't have it. His heart lurched. *Clarke.* He needed to find her before she did something well-meaning and reckless.

Bellamy gritted his teeth and began crawling forward on his stomach. He glanced up and saw Wells and Eric sprint out of the forest. They grabbed an injured Earthborn from the ground and dragged him toward the edge of the clearing to take shelter in the trees. Bellamy sprang to his feet and ran over to them, crouching next to Eric and Wells behind a large tree.

"Have you seen Clarke or Octavia?" Bellamy asked hoarsely.

Wells shook his head.

"Has anyone seen Felix?" Eric asked, leaning forward to peer into the clearing.

"He's hiding under a table," Bellamy said. "I was with him a moment ago. He was okay."

Eric let out a long breath. "Thank god."

"What the hell is going on?" Bellamy asked, the words spilling out though he knew he wouldn't get a real answer. He could see his own confusion and terror mirrored in Eric's and Wells's faces.

"I don't know," Wells said, a note of anguish in his voice. "Wait . . . look there . . ."

On the opposite side of the clearing, people emerged from the shadows of the forest. There were at least two dozen of them, all male. They had shaved heads and wore all white. And they were *marching*.

Bellamy's blood turned to ice as the figures moved closer, their expressionless, masklike faces coming into chilling focus. But nothing was as terrifying as the guns glinting in the late-afternoon sun.

As they moved toward the center of the clearing, a few of the men broke from formation to yank Colonists and Earthborns out from under the tables. They dragged the people away by their arms and legs, and headed back toward the woods with their captives.

"What are they doing? We can't let them *take* anyone," Wells said. He stood up and lunged forward, but not before Bellamy and Eric each took hold of a shoulder.

"Are you crazy?" Bellamy hissed. "They'll *kill* you."

"We can't just hide. Look what they're doing!" Wells wrenched away from Bellamy and Eric, and pointed with a shaking hand. Another group of the white-clad men marched out of the supply cabin, carrying large canvas sacks. The bastards were taking all their supplies, their food, their wood stores. Even the weapons they were using looked familiar, and for good reason. The intruders had stolen the Colonists' rifles to use against them.

A hand on Bellamy's shoulder made him jump. It was Clarke's father, ashen and trembling. But it wasn't his pale face that made Bellamy's pulse stutter. He had one arm wrapped around his wife, who was clutching her side, her hands drenched in slick red.

"Are you okay?" Bellamy asked as Wells hurried to take her arm.

"I'm fine," Mary said, though her face was contorted in pain. "But I'm worried about Clarke. She was on her way to the infirmary when the explosions started. I don't know . . ." She trailed off with a grimace.

"I'll find her." Bellamy reached out to squeeze her uninjured arm. "I promise."

"I'll come with you," Wells said.

"No, you stay with them." Bellamy nodded toward Clarke's parents. "Then you'll be closer to the injured people." He prayed that there'd still be people left to help when this thing was over.

The expressionless, white-clad men had spread out through the clearing. Some kicked the bodies on the ground, searching for signs of life. It was unclear to Bellamy who they were looking for, what determined who they left and who they dragged away. Every few moments, another ear-ringing shot ran out, followed by screams, or worse, silence.

Bellamy turned and ran through the woods toward the infirmary cabin at the other end of the clearing. Months of hunting had taught him to move quickly and silently, though this time, he wasn't the hunter—he was the prey. He passed a number of people huddled behind the trees, watching him wide-eyed as he sprinted by. A few called to him, but he didn't break stride. First he had to make sure Clarke and his sister were safe. Then he'd do whatever he could to help the others.

"Bel?" came a loud whisper. A flash of black hair tied in that ragged red ribbon. *Octavia.*

He skidded to a stop. His sister was crouched behind a bush near the edge of the clearing, her arms curved out to pen in as many of the children as she could, keeping them from wiggling into view of the invaders. "What do we do?" she asked quietly, her voice full of more fierceness than fear.

"Stay there," Bellamy said quietly. "I'll come back for you."

Octavia nodded, whispering to the children.

Bellamy was nearly at the infirmary cabin, but he'd have to dash across open ground to get there. Thankfully, the invaders hadn't come up this far; they were still concentrated at the other end of the clearing near the supply cabins, where the feast had been laid out.

Bellamy let out a long, ragged breath when he reached the door. The cabin looked untouched, no invaders in sight. But it was worryingly silent.

A branch cracked behind him and Bellamy whirled around, fists clenched. But instead of one of the men in white, it was a Colony guard, arms raised in surrender. Luke was almost unrecognizable, covered in gray soot from his curly hair to his boots. He held a rifle, which he lowered as he took a few steps toward Bellamy, limping more than usual.

Bellamy clapped a hand on Luke's arm. "You all right?"

Luke looked more bewildered than scared. "I got thrown by the first blast, then somebody, one of those guys in white, started dragging me before the second one went off. I got away, got this gun, and fought them off."

Bellamy glanced around. "Were you followed?"

"I don't think so."

"Good. Come on. Let's get inside."

Bellamy tried to open the infirmary door and found it barricaded with cabinets, medical bags, and cots. *Good thinking, Clarke*, he thought, even if it was keeping them out too. But they'd need to hurry. The invaders were still focused on raiding supplies from the other end of the clearing, but they'd make their way to this end soon enough. "Clarke," he called softly. "It's me."

Clarke's fingers appeared at the top of the pile, pulling objects downward. "You'll need to climb!" she called. "I'll make room at the top. Who's with you? Do you have the kids?"

"They're hiding with O," Bellamy called back. "We'll bring them here."

"Go!" Clarke said, but Bellamy was already running back toward the perimeter, Luke on his tail.

Smoke poured out of the camp's decimated buildings, and a huge gray cloud billowed over the new residential cabins. In the moments that he'd been at the infirmary, the men in white seemed to have left the clearing.

The kids must have seen Bellamy and Luke coming, because the littlest of them started to creep out from the relative safety of the woods. Bellamy cursed. The camp might look eerily empty now, but they'd been under attack just minutes ago. The boy, maybe five, ran toward Luke, sobbing, arms extended to be picked up. But they were still three hundred yards away, minimum. The other kids followed the boy in a mad rush, all order abandoned.

Bellamy broke into a sprint, pointing the children toward the infirmary as they passed him in a wave, his eyes scanning the edge of the clearing so fast everything seemed to blur.

Everything but Octavia, still too far away, stumbling as she ran. Then, like a scene from a nightmare, three tall figures in white emerged from the shadow of the woods. Bellamy could only run and run and run and watch, his eyes boring into his sister's face.

Run, he shouted. Except that no sound came out. Not even when two of the men grabbed her, wrenching her arms behind her back, while the third pulled a syringe from his pocket and plunged it into her neck. A few seconds later, she fell limp as a cloth doll into her captors' arms.

"No!" Bellamy screamed. "Get your hands off of her; I will *kill* you!"

The three figures glanced up, blandly curious; then one of them tossed something into the clearing between them— and the others carried his sister back into the woods.

Bellamy started to chase them, but Luke grabbed hold of him and dragged him backward.

"It's a grenade. Get down!"

They fell beside each other on the hard ground, hands over their heads, bracing for the blast, but it was a muffled one. Bellamy peered up, seeing a wall of smoke between him and the last spot he'd seen his sister. He pulled up his shirt, covering his face and holding his breath as he tore through the fog, emerging on the other side to see . . . nothing.

The invaders were gone.

And so was Octavia.

CHAPTER *5*

Wells

Something thudded against his head, over and over in a slow, relentless rhythm. He tried to open his eyes, but they were as heavy as sandbags and something gnawed at the back of his mind, whispering that he didn't want to wake up quite yet. He wasn't ready to know.

The last he could remember, he'd been in the woods with Eric. Bellamy had gone to find Clarke, and Wells and Eric were darting in and out of the clearing, grabbing more injured and bringing them to the woods, where Clarke's father could treat them. He and Eric had just ducked back under the cover of the trees, supporting someone between them. Then there had been a sharp sting against his shoulder blade. Wells had turned to find a strange, unsmiling man with sunken cheeks. Then . . . nothing.

Awareness crept in. The feel of hard, cracked wood beneath his shoulders. A swaying motion, like he'd felt on the dropship before it hit Earth's atmosphere. A sour humid smell; a weird grinding sound. Light flickered past his eyelids.

"This one's waking up," said a voice beside his ear, male, unfamiliar.

Wells's eyes flew open. He was staring at a wooden wall, badly built, with gaps between the thin, rotting boards. Through one of the gaps, he could see a green blur. His bleary mind began to put pieces together, agonizingly slowly. The forest? They were moving through it. This was some sort of vehicle.

"Watch him," came another, deeper voice, farther away.

"Where the hell are you taking us?" a familiar voice shouted. There was a loud thump, the wall rattling. A face rose up in Wells's mind, a smug smirk, and then a name. Graham. The screaming boy was Graham.

"He's not ready yet. Give him another shot," came the deep voice again.

Startled, Wells shifted, but realized his arms were bound behind him, maybe his ankles too. It was hard to tell—his spine was coiled and cramped, his legs numb. He kicked, just a little, and his legs erupted in excruciating pinpricks.

"You're all right," came that same, affectless voice above him. Wells managed to turn his head just far enough to see a pale boy staring down at him. "The fight's over. You're one of the lucky ones."

"The lucky ones?" Wells tried to say, but his mouth wouldn't work.

I've been drugged. The pain in my back . . . they caught me in the woods and injected me with something.

"You're one of us now," the pale boy said, looking away. "If you don't scream, we'll let you wake up."

But Wells hardly heard the end of that sentence. He was slipping again and then gone.

It was dark the next time he opened his eyes. Someone had propped him into a sitting position, his legs stretched out in front of him, still bound by thick twine. Holding his breath, he blinked until his vision adjusted. His earlier guess had been right. He was inside a covered wagon of some sort, with tall wooden walls and high, barred windows. There was a little bench on the other side of the narrow space. Three men in white uniforms sat on it, including the pale boy and the frightening man from the woods. Wells inhaled sharply, but they weren't looking at him. They weren't talking to one another either, just sitting there, rocking with the movement of the cart, their eyes completely blank.

The road lurched and Wells's shoulder bumped against someone else's. His body still wasn't as responsive as he wished, but he managed to turn his head enough to get a view of four people beside him. They were all bound to the wall in seated positions, all asleep, probably drugged. Wells's heart gave a lurch as his eyes passed over their faces. Next to Graham was Eric, a deep gash on one cheek, followed by an Arcadian kid. The fourth still figure was a little older, less familiar. It was one of Sasha's people.

Another knot formed in his already clenched stomach. No matter what he did, he continued to let her down. He didn't know who these murderers in white were, but they hadn't shown up on the scene until the Colonists appeared.

Wells had suspected there must be other people alive on Earth, but Sasha's people had never encountered any others. Had they found their site because of the dropships? Had the Colonists doomed them all?

The cart jolted and his head rolled back. He drew a breath and righted it, cricking his neck straight again.

The pale soldier was staring at him across the dark wagon. Wells stared back.

"Who are you?" Wells asked, and this time sound actually came out.

"We're the Protectors," the boy said in a strange, almost dreamy voice.

"*Protectors*," Wells spat as he recalled the smoke from the explosions. The bodies on the ground. "You tried to kill us. Who the hell are you and what do you want?"

"We raided your camp," the boy said calmly. "We took what was useful and discarded what wasn't. You'll learn."

Panic rose in Wells's chest, but he wrestled it down. "If you just needed supplies, why did you take us with you?"

The boy's icy blue eyes fixed Wells with an appraising glare. "You may be useful. Or you may not. We'll know soon. It doesn't take long to weed out the weak."

Wells refused to look away, the feat of holding in his rage made that much easier by whatever drug they'd injected him with, still wending its way out of his system.

The older man who'd seized Wells nodded. "You're young. Strong," he said. "If Earth wills it, you'll do just fine."

The other two repeated dully, "If Earth wills it."

Wells heard a gasp down the line. He swiveled his head to see Eric starting to wake up. Eric blinked a few times; then his eyes widened. His jaw twitched like he was about to start yelling, but Wells shook his head a tiny bit, praying Eric was lucid enough to pick up the signal.

He was. Eric swallowed, blinking once in reply, and lowered his eyes to the floor. *Good*, Wells thought. *I need time to get more answers.*

"Where are you taking us?" Wells asked, trying to stay calm.

"You'll like it there," the third man, reedy and tall, said. Wells hadn't heard him speak before. His voice was strangely sweet, lyrical, almost like he was reciting a nursery rhyme. "It's the safest place."

"The safest place where?" Wells asked, unable to hold back a note of frustration.

"The safest place on Earth," the man said, smiling. "One day it will all be safe, if Earth wills it."

"If Earth wills it," they all said again, sending shivers down Wells's back.

"And if you're chosen, you will help us spread peace," the pale soldier said.

"So you're peacekeepers?" Wells said.

"We're *raiders*," said the older man. "And so will you be if you learn to keep your mouth shut."

"I thought you called yourselves Protectors," Wells said carefully. They all turned to stare at him for a long moment.

The sweet-voiced man smiled. "You'll learn."

He tried another tack. "How did you find our camp?"

"It's not your camp anymore," the older man said sharply. "It's not your village either. Can't have a village without Earth's blessing."

"So you destroyed it, and killed everyone in your way," Eric said, his voice raw with pain. He was fully awake now and quivering with rage.

"We didn't kill *everyone*," the pale boy said, his eyes wide as if shocked. "We're not monsters. We do Earth's work, that's all. We spared the strongest of you and kept the best of your women, didn't we?"

Wells and Eric exchanged terrified glances. Who else had they taken? He prayed with every fiber in his body that they weren't talking about Clarke, Octavia, or Glass. Or, his stomach churned, one of the younger girls like Molly.

"And we left the young and the weak." The pale boy leaned forward, still protesting. "We didn't *kill* them. Earth will do with them as She sees fit."

The young. The weak. Wells's heart raced as he thought about the infirmary, praying Clarke had been in there—one of the *discarded* they'd left behind when they'd raided the camp. But what about Bellamy? And Max?

"Why are you doing this?" came a husky, lilting voice at the end of the row. The Earthborn villager had woken up. He was staring at the soldiers, his eyes glittering with tears. "Why did you destroy what we worked so hard to build?"

The boy blinked, apparently confused by the question. "Because it was the right thing to do. It's what we do everywhere."

"Everywhere?" Wells repeated.

"Everywhere that's left," he said, gazing away out the dark, barred window. "Until all of Earth is safe."

"Safe from *what*?" Wells snapped, unable to stop himself.

"You'll learn," said the older man, the one who'd taken him, as the others droned together, "You'll learn."

Wells clenched his fists behind him, settling in for the long ride. One way or another, these "raiders," "Protectors," whatever they were, were right—Wells *was* going to learn. He would learn as much as he possibly could.

And then he would fight back.

CHAPTER *6*

Clarke

The red Hunter's Moon had come and gone, the sun had risen on a new day, and the camp was still burning. A slow billow of smoke streamed up from the scorched earth, covering the sky in a sickly gray fog. But it did nothing to obscure what was left of the camp.

As Clarke stepped out of the infirmary cabin for a breath of air, she tried to brace herself for the devastation, but the scene before her was still like a punch to the gut. In addition to the guard tower, more than half of the newly built cabins had been destroyed. The clearing was strewn with pieces of charred wood, mangled bits of metal, and scraps of clothing. And until a few hours ago . . . bodies.

Whoever had attacked them had vanished as quickly and mysteriously as they'd appeared, but there was no pretending that yesterday's events had been a terrible dream. At sunset, twenty-two bodies would be lowered into freshly dug graves. Now Clarke, her father, and Dr. Lahiri were doing everything in their power to make sure that number didn't rise, that all of the injured stayed with them . . . including her mother.

As she turned toward the section of camp where the residential cabins used to stand, the horizon rippled with waves of heat. They'd tried to douse the fires at first, but the Council had called an end to it. Clarke understood. They had only a few things left: water and a tiny bit of reserve energy. There was no sense in wasting both of them on a losing battle, especially since the wind was faint and the flames were no longer spreading. One of the smoldering cabins had become a makeshift bonfire. The beds in the infirmary were strictly for the injured, so Clarke wasn't surprised to see people huddled around the cabin, warming themselves.

We'll need food, Clarke thought dimly, rubbing her eyes, which itched from smoke. Last night, they'd checked the camp's food stores, knowing what they'd find. Everything they'd stocked up for winter had been taken by the raiders. Bellamy would have to take a hunting party out soon.

But the food, weapons, and wood stores were meaningless compared to what else had been stolen. The dead and wounded were all accounted for, which meant that nineteen people were missing. No one past middle age had been taken—and thankfully all the children were safe—but that was little comfort to their friends and family. One woman had to be physically restrained from going after the daughter she'd seen dragged away. To Clarke's surprise, Bellamy had been one of the people to hold her back, even though they'd taken Octavia and Wells. Even in his frenzied haze of fury and pain, he'd realized the futility of going after their attackers unprepared and unarmed.

Clarke stepped over a charred log, once the lintel of the guards' barracks, and ran numbers in her head. Around two hundred currently safe or only slightly injured. Nearly thirty gravely injured. Twenty-two dead. Nineteen missing.

Octavia. Glass. Graham. Eric. *Wells.* Her best friend. Her first love. The boy who'd risked everything to protect her.

Clarke's breath stuttered. She pressed her hands to her knees, drawing in a shaky gasp, willing the sob that was rising in her throat to stay put. Not now. Not yet. Not until they'd done all they could to help the injured, soothe the dying, ready the camp for another long night . . . and figure out what to do next. Clarke retied her ponytail and turned back toward the infirmary.

Then a distant voice stopped her. Bellamy.

Clarke turned to see him in quiet conversation with Rhodes and Max beside the dwindling bonfire. His back was to her, head bowed. She'd hardly laid eyes on him all day. He'd been too busy patrolling and taking stock of the camp to come by the infirmary. Or maybe he'd been avoiding her.

Part of her wanted to keep walking to avoid having to look into his pained eyes. She should've trusted him, should've believed him, instead of writing off his concerns as paranoia. He was one of the smartest, most intuitive people she'd ever met, and yet she'd treated him like a disturbed patient.

She headed toward the bonfire, the shame in her chest burning hotter than the flames. As she neared the small group, their conversation became audible.

"What else?" Max was asking.

"Heaped piles of leaves," Bellamy said, motioning to the woods. "And when Luke and I scouted this morning, we confirmed what I'd suspected. There were holes dug under the leaf piles. They may have hid supplies there for the attack. Or themselves, even. Makeshift bunkers."

"And you previously heard voices in the trees?" Max asked.

Clarke froze as Bellamy drew a deep breath, his shoulders rising with it.

3

"Yeah, last week. All I heard was one sentence. Two words. 'This one.' And then a whistle from another tree, and that was it. I looked up into the trees for what felt like an hour, but I couldn't see a damn thing."

"I wish you'd come to us sooner," Rhodes said. Then, maybe at Bellamy's expression, he winced, stepping back a hair. "But yes. I certainly understand."

"You have a theory?" Max cut in, nodding to Bellamy.

Bellamy straightened, adjusting his bow strap. "I think they've been watching us for the past month, maybe longer. They knew all our plans. Our routines. They knew the layout of all the buildings and when they'd be unguarded. And . . ." His voice broke slightly. "They knew who they were going to kill and who they were going to take."

"You think they were planning to take you?" Max asked.

"If I'd happened to be an easier target . . . yeah, I think so."

Even from here, Clarke could hear the bitter longing in his voice. He *wished* he'd been taken so he could be with his siblings and do his best to protect them. Bellamy sighed and looked around the clearing, his eyes landing on Clarke.

His jaw tightened, and for a brief moment, she thought he was going to ignore her. *He blames me*, she thought. *Of course he does. All of this is my fault.* But then he let out a long breath, nodded good-bye to Rhodes and Max, and came over to join her.

She braced herself for a blast of anger from him, but he clasped her shoulders and pulled her into an embrace. The warmth of his skin, the weight of his arms, unlocked something inside her. All the fear and guilt she'd been desperately holding back came rushing forward, and soon tears were streaming down her cheeks. Once they started, she couldn't seem to get them to stop.

"Are you okay?" Bellamy whispered in her ear.

Sobs wracked her body, and for a few moments, she couldn't speak. Could barely breathe. She fell into him and he tightened his hold, stroking her hair.

Finally, she took a step back and wiped her face with the back of her hand. "I'm so sorry," she said hoarsely. "*You knew*, Bellamy. You knew the whole time and I didn't listen. I wish there were better words, but all I can say is that I'm sorry. I'm *an idiot*. I'm—"

"No, Clarke." Bellamy grabbed her hand. "No. This is not your fault. It's theirs. Whoever they are."

She shook her head so viciously it hurt. "I should have trusted you."

"Yeah." He shut his eyes briefly and sighed. "Yes, okay, I agree. You should have. But you know what? I'm not sure I would have either, if I'd been in the same position. We're all just doing the best we can."

Bellamy drew her in again, pressing his hand against

her back, solid and forgiving, even when he had no reason to be.

Clarke rested her cheek against his chest, allowing herself one moment to close her eyes, but when she opened them again and peered up at Bellamy, he was looking out past her at the forest, his brow lined with worry. She could hear his heart thudding too fast.

He wanted to get out of here. To find his brother and sister, and hurt the people who took them. Bellamy didn't have time for anger. There was only time for action.

All this death, destruction, loss could have been prevented if she'd just done the one thing she'd promised Bellamy to do: to have his back. To be his partner. To listen. But Bellamy was right. It was done. All Clarke could do now was try to be better from this point on.

She pulled softly away, wiped her cheeks with one last sniff, and nodded up at him. "What's next?"

He pointed toward Max and Rhodes, who were rounding up a few guards and other familiar faces. "We're about to announce our plan."

CHAPTER 7

Bellamy

The surviving Colonists and Earthborns clustered around the bonfire, shooting nervous glances toward the woods.

We're not safe anywhere, Bellamy thought bitterly as he joined Max and the other members of the Council in the center of the crowd. They were one short: An Arcadian woman named Fiona, who'd established herself as a wise and warm presence during her short time on Earth, was now lying in the expanding cemetery.

Max raised his hand and the murmurs died away, leaving an uneasy silence. Bellamy shifted his weight from side to side. Every minute they spent discussing the situation was another minute wasted. He didn't have time for this.

He needed to go *now*. He had half a mind to head out on his own, but then his eyes traveled across the crowd and landed on the group of children that had all been rescued safely, most of them clinging to Molly, who at thirteen was now the oldest of their group. They were all looking at Bellamy, eyes wide and shining with something that looked strangely more like hope than fear.

They trust me, he realized. *They don't see me as a former criminal who keeps screwing up. They're counting on me.*

Rhodes nodded to Max, stepped forward, and began to speak. The sound of his voice still set Bellamy's teeth on edge. Though they were on the same side now, it would take more time than a couple of months to undo the bone-deep resentment Bellamy felt toward him. Still, there were more important things to focus on right now . . . like finding and destroying the bastards who'd taken Wells and Octavia.

"I know that you're all hoping for answers about what happened to us last night," Rhodes said. "I'll start with what we do *not* know. We do not know who attacked us."

The crowd grumbled, anxiety rippling through them in a wave.

"But we will find out," Rhodes cut in, raising a hand to quiet them. "We do not know what their motivation for attacking us was, beyond stealing our supplies. *But we will find out.*"

His voice was firmer now, and the crowd was with him. Even Bellamy found himself nodding along.

"We do not know why they took our people, but believe me when I tell you that we will find out." He smiled grimly, an unspoken promise of revenge lingering under his words. The crowd was hushed. "We do not know where they took our people . . . but we now know *how* to find out." Rhodes backed up a step, motioning Bellamy forward. "My fellow Councilor Bellamy Blake led a small scouting party into the forest this morning."

The murmurs returned, but this time, they contained a note of surprise and admiration. Bellamy cleared his throat.

"The people who attacked our camp were skilled at hiding their plans," Bellamy started, "but they were a lot sloppier about covering up their tracks."

He scanned the crowd and found Luke leaning against a tree on the far side. He'd been with Bellamy when they found the telltale wagon ruts leading away from camp. Bellamy tried to catch his eye, but Luke was staring off into the distance, his dazed look a stark contrast to his usual alert, focused expression. Bellamy knew exactly what he was feeling. He'd seen the agony in Luke's face when he'd told Bellamy that Glass had been taken.

Bellamy pointed toward the dimming eastern sky. "The

attackers took our friends that way, due east. There were no signs of struggle or violence, so we've got to assume they were captured unharmed for a reason."

His stomach clenched saying it. Octavia had to be alive. Wells too. They had to be, or else the fire keeping him alive would go out, and he'd disintegrate into ash.

"We have a trail," he went on, more firmly. "And we had some weapons still at Mount Weather. Not many, but enough to give us a fighting chance. Tonight, I'm going to head out with a small group of volunteers. We're going to find the bastards who took our people and we're going to bring them home."

The crowd responded with shouts of approval at first, then a low grumble rose up beneath it, and an older woman Bellamy recognized from back on Walden stepped forward, shaking her head.

"You can't take all the weapons with you. We'll be defenseless if they attack again while you're gone." A few heads nodded in agreement.

"I understand you're worried," Bellamy said, speaking loudly to make sure everyone heard. "But we only have three guns, and we'll need every one of them for our rescue mission."

"But what about us?" an Earthborn man shouted. "Why do their lives matter more than ours?"

Max stepped forward. "Bellamy and his team are going to be *following* the attackers. If, for some unknown reason, they decide they want to raid our camp a second time, Bellamy will know. They'll come back with the guns and fight for us."

"That's a ridiculous plan," the older woman said. "They need to leave at least one of the guns here. Besides, Bellamy's far and away the best hunter. Without him, we'll starve. He should stay behind."

"Like hell I will," Bellamy snapped, before he had time to stop himself.

"I assure you that there are many skilled hunters among my people," Max said, shooting Bellamy a reproachful look. "We aren't going to let anyone starve."

"Why should we trust you?" a recently arrived Phoenician woman shouted. "You were hiding weapons at Mount Weather, guns that could've been used to fight off the attackers!"

The crackling of the bonfire was soon drowned out by the buzz of heated conversation as people shouted over one another to be heard.

"That's enough!" Rhodes's voice boomed. "We'll put it to a vote. All those in favor of sending out an armed party to retrieve the members of our community who were taken in last night's attacks, raise your hands."

His words were drowned out by a chorus of "Yes" as hands flew into the air.

"All those opposed . . ."

A few hands rose up, but not enough. Bellamy felt his heart start to pound with anticipation. Now he could do what he'd been longing to since the moment he saw his sister dragged into the woods. Chase them. Find her and Wells. Get his revenge. No matter the risk.

"We have a few volunteers already," Max was saying, "and we'll be keeping the party purposely small, to avoid detection. But if anyone would like to join us, please step for—"

"I'll go," Clarke's voice called out. Bellamy's skin went cold, watching her pick her way out of the crowd, her lips set in that stubborn line that Bellamy knew meant there was no talking her out of anything. "You'll need someone with medical training with you."

No, Bellamy thought. It was one thing for him to put himself in danger, but the thought of anything happening to Clarke was more than he could bear. He opened his mouth to argue, but before he could, another voice said it for him.

"Absolutely not," Clarke's father shouted, breathing heavily as he jogged over from the direction of the infirmary.

Clarke shot her father an impatient look. Finding her parents alive had been a miracle, banishing the specter of grief that'd always clung to her. Yet while her broken heart had healed, Bellamy knew that having her parents around was a bit of an adjustment.

She took a deep breath and motioned for her father to join her a little bit away from the rest of the group. Bellamy went to stand next to them, wracking his brain for a way to support Clarke while ensuring that she stayed behind.

"Your mother and I did everything in our power to get back to you," her dad said.

"I know," Clarke replied softly.

"And now against all odds, we're finally together again. Your mother's condition is serious. She needs you here. This is the worst possible time for you to go jaunting off, straight into god knows what kind of danger."

"But we don't get to pick the timing, do we?" As Clarke took her father's hands and squeezed, Bellamy could see the anger fading from the older man's eyes. "If we could, we'd never have been attacked. You'd never have been sent down before me. We would have been together this whole time."

Clarke glanced back at Bellamy, clearly looking for backup. And though he wished she could stay here, she was right. They had no idea what condition their friends and family would be in—they'd need a medic with them. Bellamy stepped closer, in solidarity with her.

"I won't be alone," she said. "We'll be careful and smart. But we *have* to do what we can for them. I can't just sit here and do nothing. They have Wells, Dad. I can't just abandon him. That's not who I am."

Her father's shoulders slumped; then he took a deep breath and nodded once. "Just promise me you'll be careful."

Though he didn't want to put Clarke in danger, Bellamy felt strangely relieved. He was grateful to have her by his side. There was no better person to join the party: She was brilliant and brave, and an incredible problem solver. And, selfishly, he hated being apart from her, the person who made this wild, strange planet feel like home.

"I will," Clarke said. "I promise."

"And swear that you won't do anything foolish. There's a big difference between bravery and recklessness."

Clarke shot Bellamy a look, as if to say that he needed that advice more than she did. Despite himself, Bellamy smiled.

"Yes, I understand that," Clarke said.

"You're leaving tonight?" Clarke's father asked.

Bellamy nodded. "We can't risk waiting until tomorrow and losing the trail. We need to leave soon. *Now.*" He glanced around the clearing, anxiously tapping his foot. "Why is Luke just standing there? We have to get moving." He cleared his throat. "Luke . . . Luke! What the—" He cut himself off as Clarke squeezed his arm, her expression slightly pained.

Too distressed to notice the exchange, David Griffin let out a long sigh. "Okay. Be sure to say good-bye to your mother before you head out. And you"—he locked eyes with Bellamy—"take care of her."

"I promise," Bellamy said. "Though I think we both know she can take care of herself." He glanced over at Clarke. In the late-afternoon sun, her hair shined like gold. Combined with the intensity of her glowing green eyes, she looked fierce and otherworldly, like some ancient goddess of war.

Clarke's father gave a grim smile. "I know." He turned and walked away, suddenly looking older and more tired than he had minutes earlier.

Bellamy laced his fingers between Clarke's, holding tight. He was glad she was coming with him. They were stronger together. Always had been.

She squeezed his hand and then let go. "I'd better say good-bye to my mom."

The group around the bonfire was starting to break up. A few people were distributing some meager rations for dinner, while Paul organized a crew to sort through piles of charred blankets, looking for anything salvageable. Like last night, people would have to sleep outside.

"Okay," Bellamy said. "I'm going to find Luke and get the supplies ready."

Clarke looked around the crowd. "Who else is going with us?"

"Luke, of course. And Felix. I don't think he's even sat down since Eric was taken. We'll see if he's able to calm down and focus. A couple of Earthborns. And Paul volunteered."

Bellamy grimaced slightly, and waited for Clarke to do the same, but to her surprise, she nodded. "Great." She glanced over to where Paul was sorting blankets. "He seems like he'll be useful. Steady."

Something about the world rankled Bellamy. "Steady?" he repeated.

Clarke shrugged and tried to play it off like it was nothing, but as she walked away, he caught a glimpse of something in her eye. Worry. Fear. But not just about the people who'd been taken.

She was still worried about him. Still didn't know if he'd recovered enough to be trusted. And the worst part was that he wasn't sure she was wrong.

CHAPTER 8

Glass

At first, when Glass and the seven other girls had woken up, they'd shouted until they'd lost their voices. Their screams got them nothing; their captors stayed silent, their masklike faces betraying no emotion. Their wagon just kept onward, all night and into the early morning, stopping only occasionally for breaks. All Glass knew was that they were following a bumpy trail through the middle of a dense forest.

She didn't know the other prisoners very well. Octavia was with her, and a pretty Earthborn girl named Lina. The other five were almost strangers. But they were a unit, bound together by their despair.

And thankfully, she knew that Luke was alive. The last

thing she remembered was the look of helpless anguish on his face. Wherever these people were taking her, he'd come after her.

Glass fought through her exhaustion and refused to succumb to sleep. She wasn't going to miss an opportunity to gather crucial information about her captors. There was no knowing what detail would end up meaning the difference between life and death.

But her observations just made her more confused. The ground was "good." The raiders kissed their fingertips and touched the dirt every time they set foot on it after leaving the wagon. Hard work was good, judging by their constant droning conversation about it. They called themselves "Protectors." She wasn't sure where killing people fit in the grand order of good or bad, except that Earth was the best thing of all, the deity they seemed to worship, and that Earth . . . it . . . *She* . . . was the decider of who lived and who did not.

Hours passed aimlessly, the wagon rocking and the guards staring in silence. Lina sobbed uncontrollably until she eventually seemed to run out of tears. Finally, the young guard opposite Glass leaned forward, his eyes cast up, peering out of the high window.

"We're in sight," he said, then turned to the girls with a solemn frown. "Not long now, if Earth wills it."

"If Earth wills it," the others repeated.

Glass and Octavia exchanged worried looks.

The wagon made a sharp left and all the girls toppled a little, the stale smell of sweat and warm breath wafting even stronger with the movement. The guards all turned to peer out the narrow front window, past the driver's high seat. Spurred by a combination of curiosity and apprehension, Glass craned her head to see what they were all looking at.

They were approaching an ivy-covered wall that extended as high and wide as she could see. It just stretched and stretched and stretched.

The young guard saw her watching and smiled tightly at her. "We've arrived at our great home."

"Oh," Glass said, unsure how to respond.

He seemed encouraged by that. "It was here before the Shattering, when man was wicked and untamed . . . the greatest fortress in the land. The most powerful men sat there, hoarding their power, but then Earth took their power and She gave it to *us*." The chest of his white uniform swelled with pride. "Earth's magic resides within us. Soren said so."

"Soren?" Glass asked.

The guard nodded. "Soren is Earth's mouthpiece."

Soren's their leader, then, Glass thought. Another piece of information to add to the pile.

"Our great home is in the shape of a perfect pentagon," another guard said.

"We call it the Stone," the younger one cut back in. "The Stone is our new home, and if Earth wills it, it will be the foundation for our great work."

The wagon grew dark as they approached the shadow of the great gray wall. Then, with a clomping lurch, they stopped. Glass crawled forward as the back doors opened, curious for a better look, but the second her foot hit the ground, the closest guard shoved a blindfold over her face.

Glass didn't struggle. She was fully in enemy territory and the only way out was to survive long enough for the rescue party to arrive. She kept silent, and in reward, the hand on her elbow kept a gentle grip as it led her forward. To that building, she supposed. To whatever was waiting for them. To whatever she'd force herself to endure as long as necessary.

As they stepped through what felt like a doorway onto hard, flat flooring, Glass's pulse sped up, goose bumps prickling on her arms. She was inside their fortress.

The air grew warmer, staler, as they led her around one corner, then another. She couldn't keep track even now that she was trying. Then they stopped walking and pulled her blindfold from her face with a strangely dramatic flourish, as if she was meant to be impressed.

Glass blinked into the shadowy space. It was a cavern-ous, windowless room with skeletal metal posts holding up the tall ceiling every few yards, each hung with a flicker-ing lantern. Her eyes adjusted, but hardly anything came into focus, because there was hardly anything in here. Just stacked mats spaced at even intervals, some of them with girls sitting on them, unmoving, their feet flat against the cold floor, staring blankly at the new arrivals.

The young guard attempted a painful-looking smile. "The women's den. Make yourself at home."

Den? Glass thought, recoiling slightly at the odd choice of words.

They gave strange little bows, leaving their eight bewil-dered prisoners behind as they backed out of the room, shutting the door behind them.

Glass braced for the sound of a lock, and sure enough, there came the same telltale clank that'd haunted her all those terrible months in Confinement. The cruel irony produced a silent, grim laugh. She'd fled the dropship, scrambled through air ducts as a fugitive, spacewalked, and lost her mother in her struggle to make it down to Earth—and for what? Here she was, locked up again, separated from Luke by a distance much farther than the skybridge.

After the door clanked shut, the girls sitting stiffly on

the mats seemed to relax slightly, rolling their ankles and rubbing their shoulders. There were more than two dozen of them in this "den," all dressed in white dresses, their hair tied back severely in tight braids. The girl nearest her was sitting in an awkward position with her bare feet flat on the ground. And for some reason, she was scowling at Glass.

Glass tried a nervous smile. The girl didn't return it.

"You should take off your shoes," the girl snapped. "Our feet must touch Earth while we are in Her service."

Two cots over, a pretty girl with curly dark hair sighed wearily. "Look down, Bethany. Does this look like Earth to you? We're *inside*."

Glass stared at her, startled. The girl's accent wasn't like any of the Earthborns' or the Protectors'. It almost sounded like . . . but no, that was impossible . . .

But Octavia had caught it too. Her head whipped around, and she was staring at the girl, wide-eyed.

The curly-haired girl rested her feet on the mattress, in apparent violation of their "feet on the Earth" rules, and as she leaned back, the lantern light hit her face and Glass was sure she recognized her.

Glass grabbed Octavia's arm, and they walked toward her quietly. "Are you from the Colony?" Glass whispered.

The girl stood up so fast she nearly knocked Glass over. "Your accent . . . are you a *Phoenician*?"

They stared at one another, dumbfounded. Finally, Glass spoke. "How is this possible? What's your name? Where did you come from?"

"My name's Anna. I was in a dropship that went off course. I'm not sure what happened, but we crashed far away." She winced, and Glass briefly closed her eyes as memories of her own terrible crash came flashing back. "It was awful," Anna continued hoarsely. "Eleven people died on impact, and a bunch more over the next few days. It's funny. You spend your whole life being told that Earth is this paradise, and then it turns out to be one horrific nightmare after another. I wished I'd just stayed behind."

"The ship was dying," Glass said, flinching as she remembered the faces of people who realized they had nowhere to go as the air leaked out of the ships.

"I know. But at least I would've been with my family. There's nothing for me here. I hate this planet," she said bitterly.

"It's not all so bad," Glass said. A wistful note crept into her voice as she thought about walking through the woods with Luke, about waking up in his arms to the joyful trill of birdsong.

Octavia shifted closer to Anna. "So what happened after you crashed?" she asked curiously, the terror of her capture momentarily overshadowed by the strangeness of meeting a new Colonist.

"It was awful. No one could agree about what to do. We all wanted to find the rest of you, of course, but we didn't know how to get there. In the end, we split up into smaller groups, which I realize now was dumb. Together, we might've had safety in numbers. But apart, it was easy for them"—she jerked her head toward the door—"to attack. I fought as hard as I could. I even knocked out a few of one guy's teeth."

Next to her, Octavia snickered and said, "Well done."

"But it wasn't enough to get away," Anna continued. "They took me and a few of the boys I was with, and we've been here for the past few weeks." She glanced around the room warily, as if afraid of being overheard. "So what happened to you?"

Glass's stomach clenched. Had some of the boys from their camp been captured too? She prayed that Wells wasn't among them.

She listened as Octavia gave Anna the short version of their story. Glass was slightly surprised by the animation in her voice. In her experience, Octavia had always been a little reserved around strangers, which made sense once Glass learned about the childhood spent in hiding, the adolescence in the ship's care center, and the traumas she'd endured after landing on Earth.

In the dim light, Anna's eyes grew wide as Octavia spoke. "You had *cabins*? And enough food for a *feast*? That's amazing."

"We used to have cabins," Octavia said grimly. "These *Protectors* blew most of them up. Bellamy is probably losing his mind."

"Bellamy?" Anna repeated. "Is that your boyfriend?" Was Glass imagining things, or was there a hint of disappointment in her voice?

Octavia shook her head. "No. My brother."

"Your brother? You're from the Colony and you have a *brother*? You'll have to tell me all about that." Anna sat back down, patting her mat to invite the girls to sit. Octavia immediately claimed the space right beside her.

"Why are they doing this?" Glass whispered, settling onto the other end of Anna's mat. "What do they want with us?"

Anna looked around again and lowered her voice. "Well, all the girls in this room are just what they call recruits. They're people they've captured along their way here from wherever they were before this. According to the Protectors, we're here to serve Earth. Which really means to serve *them*. Cooking, cleaning, laundry. Whatever makes us *useful* . . ." Anna trailed off and bit her lip.

"So we're just servants?" Octavia asked.

"No," Anna said, her voice barely audible. "That's all I've been doing for the past few weeks, but I think there's more."

Despite the warmth of the room, Glass shivered. "What?"

"I'm not sure. When we first got here, they forced us through some sort of cleansing ritual in the river, but they said we weren't ready to become Protectors. That we wouldn't officially join their ranks until the Earth gives them permission to lay down roots. Apparently they need to have a sign from Earth that this is their new home, and then we'll pass some sort of final test to prove we're true believers. But I'm not sure what that test is, and I'm worried there's some other way we're useful to them."

Glass's stomach roiled as she looked around the room, at the girls sitting on their mats, all of them at the mercy of these unhinged people.

"I'm happy to show them just how useful I can be," Octavia said, a dangerous edge to her voice. "As I stick a knife in their backs."

"A girl after my own heart," Anna said. "Nothing I like more than a killer with a red ribbon in her hair."

Octavia brought her hand to her hair. "I told them I would strangle them with it if they so much as touched it, so they let me keep it."

Anna grinned at her. "For some reason, that doesn't surprise me."

Footsteps echoed in the distance, and Anna's face went suddenly grave and pale as she scrambled to place her feet back on the ground.

Glass and Octavia exchanged glances, the same unspoken question running through their minds. *What on earth was going on here?*

CHAPTER 9

Wells

"You run like a wounded rabbit, boy! Do you have a *thorn* in your foot? Pick up the pace!" The Protector's rancid breath in Wells's face nearly made him gag. He'd been running for what felt like an hour, and every cell in his body burned.

After a seemingly endless ride in the putrid wagon, they'd arrived this afternoon at the Stone: a five-sided fortress with crumbling walls. They weren't even given a moment to recover from the journey. After tumbling out of the wagon, they'd been marched toward a row of what looked like chemical vats. One by one, the Protectors had shoved the prisoners up and into the tanks without explanation. Eric was the first to stop yelling and realize they were submerged in nothing more than ice-cold water.

"Wash," the Protectors had shouted, and Wells had, almost gratefully. He'd felt awake, finally, alert. Then the Protectors had dragged the prisoners out, letting them air-dry in the frigid autumn wind as they walked to collect new uniforms from a pile of white clothing. Wells's new uniform still had the name "Laurent" written on the collar. He wondered who Laurent had been: A prisoner? A true believer? Or did that amount to the same thing if you were here long enough?

While the Stone looked as if it had once been a massive, enclosed complex, nature had reclaimed much of it. Hallways ended in patches of dense trees, and staircases stood on their own, leading to nowhere. There was a well-worn path around the perimeter, and that's where Wells, Eric, Graham, and the Earthborn prisoners were running now. Whether it was a game, or a punishment, or a test, Wells wasn't sure. All he knew was that he had to keep moving.

"You are running on *Earth*," the bearded Protector jogging beside him shouted, spraying spittle at Wells's shoes. "You are striking Her with your feet. Apologize!"

"I'm sorry," Wells huffed between strides. The Protectors were carrying short, blunt sticks, and he'd seen what they did with them to prisoners who didn't answer.

"You space scum abandoned Her to die. Beg Her forgiveness!"

"Please . . . forgive me . . ."

"Pledge yourself to Her service!"

Wells's legs were burning. His lungs were burning. He could barely move, let alone speak.

"I pledge—"

The Protector's fist shot out, connecting with Wells's jaw and sending him careening off to the side. His ankles threatened to give out, his whole face throbbing with hot pain, but he kept running. He had to keep running.

The Protector kept pace beside him, but finally turned his eyes away. "You're not fit for Her service. Not yet. Keep running."

A flash of movement to the left drew Wells's attention away for a moment—Graham, stumbling off the track, gripping his jaw. The Protector next to him was opening and closing his fist, so Wells was guessing they'd just gotten to the "pledge yourself" section of the script too.

A vein in Graham's neck was pulsing, his whole face turning splotchy red. Wells watched Graham's fists balling up and rising; then Wells let one of his feet catch on the other, sending him staggering straight into Graham, knocking him onto the ground.

Graham looked like he was going to pummel Wells for

a second, his eyes practically rabid. Wells had just enough time to lean close, as though he was collapsing onto Graham's ear, and hiss, "Not like this. Not without a plan," before the Protectors swooped, dragging both of them up by the armpits.

At the next bend, the path opened up onto a large, rocky clearing. Unlike the rest of the fortress, which was filled with scattered clusters of trees, this section was empty except for a wide asphalt road that led to the largest, most intact part of the enormous building.

A line of Protectors was waiting in front of the entrance with guns. Wells felt the blood rush out of his face and chest as he wondered whether he'd made a terrible mistake sending a message to Graham. He may have just gambled with his own life.

"Line up," the bearded Protector barked as they slowed to a halt.

"Where are they taking us?" Wells asked, trying to make his voice as firm and steady as possible while he watched the others ahead of him lining up to be led away.

"To *eat*," the Protector said, coughing up the word as if disgusted by it. Wells nearly sighed with relief. "And then straight back here for more. You have a problem with that?"

Wells shook his head and saluted like he was back in guard training. The Protector started to walk away, grumbling something inaudible, and Wells decided to press his luck.

"What do I call you?" he asked. The Protector turned, nothing but menace on his face, but Wells didn't flinch. "Do you have a name?"

"You don't get to hear my name," the Protector said, his nose suddenly an inch from Wells's. "If you have to call me anything, you call me *Oak*."

"Yes, sir," Wells said, but his eyes were darting to the man's collar, so close now that he could read the name written on it in crude ink: *O'Malley*. Was that this Protector's name, or that of someone who came before?

A bowl of cold oats and another grueling jog later—this one over obstacles obscured in the dark of night—Wells found himself staggering into a hole cut into the dark, endless wall of the fortress, barely in control of his legs anymore, his head lolling forward while two raiders kept him walking.

By the time he could look up, he was at the last destination of the evening: a long room lined with cages. In his current exhausted state, it took him a few shocked seconds to realize the cages weren't for animals—they were for them. In each cage, there was only enough room for a small bedroll and a bowl that Wells was pretty sure was meant to be used as a chamber pot. In addition to the guys captured from their camp—eleven total, including Wells—there were about a dozen other "recruits," people who hadn't arrived with them.

Shock reverberated through Wells. Who were these other prisoners moaning and muttering in the other cages? And where did they come from? He knew about Max's village, and the Earthborn faction who'd broken away. But clearly the Protectors had found—and raided—other societies on this planet.

"You'll bunk here until you're officially one of us," one of the Protectors shouted as the two holding Wells up shoved him inside and clanked the door shut. "Rest up. Tomorrow won't be so easy."

The lights turned off, leaving them in impenetrable darkness. Wells listened, hearing anxious breathing, someone coughing down the line, no conversation at all in that weird, flat Protector accent.

In the silence, Wells thought of the people he'd left behind. Bellamy, his brother; Clarke, not his girlfriend anymore, but still his rock; Max, as close to a father as he'd ever get again. He wondered whether they were safe, but his mind swam with possibilities, all of them too painful to contemplate, and then landed on one fundamental truth.

He would do anything to see their faces again.

He'd do anything to get up at dawn and walk through

the silent clearing to find Molly waiting for him. Listening to her chatter as she perched on a rock, watching him chop firewood. He needed to help Luke rebuild the cabins. He had to plant flowers by Sasha's grave and watch them grow. He might not have been the leader they thought he was, but he would do better. *Be* better. He would atone for the mistakes that'd led to so much suffering.

"Wells?" came a whisper no more than six inches away. Wells jumped, making his cage clang. "Are you still awake?"

It was Eric. Wells exhaled. This was the one benefit of being stored in here like cheap cargo: close proximity to the people he needed.

"I'm awake," Wells whispered back.

"Me too," came a low voice in the other direction. It was Graham, but he didn't have that usual snide ring to his voice. He sounded as though all the bravado had been leached right out of him.

Wells's pulse jumped with as much adrenaline as his body could muster. "They were stupid to put us together."

Graham let out a faint snort. "What difference does it make?"

"We're getting out of here," Wells whispered. "But it's not going to be some mad dash, all right? They have sniper rifles, grenades, god knows what else that they haven't shown us yet. The only way we're going to be able to do this in any kind of smart way is to bide our time and play along."

"With *what*?" Wells heard his cage wall rattle as Graham gripped it. "This whole 'worshipping the planet, taking over everything, *you'll learn*' bullshit?"

"Yes," Wells said. "Exactly. They act like we'd be lucky to be among them. So let's make them think we're learning."

"Like hell I am," Graham spat. "The next time they open this cage, I'm out of here. I don't care how many skulls I have to crack."

"They'd shoot you before you had the chance," Eric said wearily. "I agree with Wells. It's the only chance we have of finding a weakness and getting back home."

"What home?" Graham whispered bleakly. "What the hell is even left?"

"Felix was still alive when they got me." Eric's voice was pinched as he said his boyfriend's name. "I saw him across the field. He was helping kids run toward the infirmary. Maybe he made it. Maybe he's waiting for me."

"We're all better people down here," Wells said. "Even you, Graham. I saw you at the creek that day, teaching Keith how to fish. Coming to Earth has made us braver. Nobler. Stronger. We're not like these Protector psychos. We *know* Earth has forgiven us, but that doesn't mean our work is over. That's why we have to get out of here. That's why we have to make it back home."

There came a little shuffle, as if Graham was sitting up. He sighed, and then after a long pause, he said, "Fine, you win, mini-Chancellor. If you think we need to play along . . . I'll play along. And we'll take these bastards down while we're at it."

"If Earth wills it," Eric said, a smile in his hushed voice.

"If Earth wills it," Wells repeated with a snort.

Wells curled onto his scratchy bedroll, his heart pounding with fatigue and fear, but finally laced with a tiny drop of hope.

CHAPTER *10*

Bellamy

Eight bags sat in a row in the afternoon heat, tidily stuffed with supplies, ready to be hoisted and carried away down the long, uncertain road.

Bellamy surveyed the contents of his bag and started to unpack it. Dried meat, apples, a hunk of cheese, half a loaf of charred bread, and a rolled woven cloth for bedding all went in a neat pile that he would return to the people remaining at camp. The only things Bellamy required were his bow and a quiver of arrows, along with one small leather canteen for storing water they sourced along the way. No need for a bedroll. He had his own small hunting knife, and any food they needed, he could hunt and forage for along the way.

"Come on everybody," Paul shouted, clapping in slow, maddening rhythm. "Bags up, feet on the ground, no time like the present."

Bellamy turned away and rubbed his temples. If this idiot kept talking this loudly, the raiders would pounce on them the second they set foot on the trail.

Some of the children poked their heads out of the lean-to he'd helped cobble together. One small girl rubbed her eyes with a confused frown and stared at him. Bellamy gave a wave and she smiled shyly back, then ran out as fast as she could, hopping back and forth on chilly bare feet.

Bellamy picked up an apple to offer to the girl if she promised she would share it, but she was already crooking a finger for him to come closer. He grinned and cocked an ear for her to speak into.

"Are you going to find Octavia?" she whispered.

"I sure am," he said, rocking back to look into her eyes, smiling through the jolt of pain shooting through his chest.

She leaned over to whisper again, "Will you tell her we love her and we miss her and we want her to come home?"

"I'll do better than that," Bellamy said. "I'll bring her back myself."

Before he had time to blink, he felt little arms wrapping themselves around his neck in a warm squeeze. Then the girl flitted away like a bird and disappeared back into the tent.

With a sigh, Bellamy stood and turned to see Clarke at the end of the row of bags, unpacking her food to leave behind, just as he had. She held a bright purple apple up to him with a rueful smile and put it aside. He grinned back, then felt it fade as Paul came stomping up.

"Do you really think it's a good idea to be rearranging our bags right now? We've got to get going."

"I'm all done," Bellamy said, standing up, pleased to note that he was a good two inches taller than Paul. "Just ensuring that our people don't starve to death while we're gone."

Paul didn't seem to note the sarcasm in his voice. "You're leaving your food behind?"

"We don't need all this," Clarke piped up, waving to her own discarded supplies. "We'll be quicker with lighter packs, don't you think?"

"Good thinking, Griffin," Paul said, placated. Bellamy rolled his eyes.

The other members of the expedition were waiting at the edge of the clearing. There had been over twenty volunteers, but Max and Rhodes had whittled the group down to eight key members. Along with Bellamy, Clarke, Luke, Paul, and Felix, there were three Earthborns known to be skilled fighters, foragers, and trackers. A young woman named Vale, a stocky man named Cooper with a scar across his cheek, and a girl a little older than Bellamy, Jessa, whose brother Kit, a Councilor, was among those taken by the raiders.

At first, Rhodes and Max had expressed concern about Luke's limp, but he'd refused to back down. "With all due respect, Councilors, I'm one of the best marksmen we have," he'd said with impeccable politeness. "And I'm not putting this rifle down until I've used it to rescue Glass."

And then there was Paul. He wasn't close to any of the people who'd been taken, but he'd still felt it was his duty to volunteer because he'd been an officer back on the ship. Like anyone gave a shit about that anymore. "I'm the only one of us who's been east of here," Paul had argued—loudly, of course. "I know the terrain, I know the challenges. I got my people from there to here, I can get these people from here to there."

Bellamy wanted to slip away without much fanfare. The quieter, the better. He heaved his pack over his shoulders, and for a brief, foolish moment, thought about picking Clarke's up for her. But then he pictured the flash of indignation that would light up her green eyes and thought better of it. She was a thousand times tougher than he was anyway. He shook Max's hand, nodded at Rhodes, and started to head across the tree line, when he heard Paul clear his throat.

"Here we are. The brave eight, walking into danger because it's the right thing to do. We don't know what we're going to find at the end of this road, but I know . . ." He pressed a fist to his heart, jaw clenched. "I have *faith* that we will overcome it and bring our friends home. When my dropship landed and everyone was consumed with worry and despair, do you know what I said to them? I said—"

"Let's save the end of that fascinating anecdote for later, Paul," Bellamy cut in. "It's time to head out."

Paul shook his head. "We can't just head into the woods willy-nilly. We need to march in *formation*."

"Formation?" Bellamy repeated, willing his blood to stop boiling.

"It's how we do it in the guard corps. Here's what I suggest: I take the advance position, in case we run into trouble. Everybody else pairs up behind me."

"We're an even number," Bellamy said dryly. "There aren't enough of us to pair—"

"I know that," Paul said quickly. "Luke takes the rear, protecting the flank."

"This is ridiculous," Bellamy said, no longer trying to hide his anger. He counted off on his fingers. "For one thing, Luke taking the flank is a terrible idea." He glanced at Luke with an apologetic wince. "No offense, man, but your leg isn't healed yet. You'll lag with that limp." He turned back to Paul. "And second, no way you should lead. Do you know how to follow a nearly dead track through a forest, day and night? Do you know what to look for? The way grass bends from a foot hitting it versus a hoof? The way rocks show mud when they've been overturned? Is that something you're familiar with?"

Paul stayed silent, his mouth clenched shut.

Bellamy nodded. "It doesn't have to be me." He pointed to Cooper, Vale, and Jessa. "They've got even more experience hunting than I do. But I'm telling you right now, it makes zero sense for you to be the guy in front. You'll lead us around in circles."

"Circles?" Paul's voice had lost some of its cheeriness. "Might I remind you that I was a senior officer back on the ship? I think that entitles me to a little respect, especially from someone who—"

Clarke cut him off. "Here's what we're going to do. Bellamy will go on ahead of us, marking the way we go and making the path a little easier to follow. That way, you can stay in the front line to protect the rest of us, Paul. And since you won't have to worry about orienteering, you can figure out where we stop to rest and make camp and look out for potential dangers, since you know the terrain so well. Luke will flank you with his rifle, providing cover for the rest of us." She paused and scanned the group, giving

them the chance to interject. When no one did, she continued. "I'm happy to take the rear. That way, if anyone needs
my medical help, I won't have to backtrack."

"That sounds logical," Paul said, smiling a little too
widely and making Bellamy's stomach churn. "I second
the motion."

"No one put it to a vote," Felix said under his breath.

Bellamy was already starting to turn away. They'd
already wasted too much time talking. It was time to leave.
The moon was full tonight and would provide plenty of
light, but if those clouds in the distance rolled in, they'd
be screwed.

Bellamy walked until the quiet of the forest surrounded
him, his eyes adjusting to the muted light. They landed on
the crossed branches, the subtle marks of wheel ruts left in
the piled leaves beyond.

Here we go, he thought, and followed the trail, heart
pounding. *Let's do it. Let's bring our people home.*

CHAPTER *11*

Clarke

As silly as keeping to formation had seemed at first, Clarke didn't mind walking in the back. She could take in the new terrain, forests opening onto wide green fields full of plants she'd never seen, before the trail took them back down into smaller, sparser copses of trees and out again. Keeping pace behind the others helped draw her mind off one reality and onto this one—one foot landing in front of the other, forward progress, a sense of hope in the middle of hopeless circumstances.

"Circumstances" sounded much nicer than "brutal, devastating attack that you completely failed to prevent."

The Earthborn members of the rescue party took turns

hanging back and keeping Clarke company. Right now, it was tall, wiry Jessa, who was a little quieter than the others. Clarke didn't mind the silence, but she noticed how the older girl's eyes were fixed on the horizon, a furrow of worry dug into her brow.

"How old is your brother?" Clarke asked gently.

Jessa cleared her throat. "A few years older than me. Kit can handle himself," she said, so sharply and suddenly, it was clear she was speaking more to herself than to Clarke. "He might not even need rescuing. But he's the only family I've got, and just going on without him like he never existed is not an option. You help the people you love. That's what you do."

"I know what you mean," Clarke said, her mind drifting to Bellamy. Since they'd set out from camp a few hours ago, he'd been too far ahead on the track for her to see him. She knew what was pulling him onward in such a frenzy, and it wasn't just the raiders' trail. It was his family. He'd spent his life protecting Octavia, and he and Wells had just started connecting as brothers. It was no wonder that he was desperate to get them back.

Clarke understood that fierce, desperate longing to find those who had been lost. She'd felt that for her parents, even when there was no logic to it, and against all odds, they'd returned to her.

At the thought of her parents, Clarke gritted her teeth against a wave of shame.

She'd spent the hours before they left by her mother's side. Dr. Lahiri's treatment seemed to be working well for her infection, and the bullet hadn't pierced any organs, but she would still have a difficult recovery ahead. Sitting with her, chatting in low voices while holding hands, Clarke had nearly reversed her decision to leave. But then her mother had murmured, "I'm proud of you. I'm proud of what you've become," and Clarke had known she meant her courage in setting out with the others. Still, her heart felt torn in two directions with every step she took away from home.

Nothing will happen to me, she promised herself. *I'll come back to them safe and sound, just as I told them I would.*

The woods broke apart as the ground grew steep under their feet. The sun was starting to set, bathing everything before her in gold.

"What the—" Ahead of her, Paul ducked as a thick vine unwound itself from a tree branch. It stretched into the air, bright yellow leaves unfurling. Clarke knew from previous investigations that the leaves were sticky, and by morning, they would be covered with insects for the vine to absorb.

"You okay?" Clarke called.

"Yeah," he said, pausing to let her catch up with him,

and he turned from side to side, slightly dazed. "What was that?"

"I've been calling them nocturnal carnivorous vines. But I have no idea what they're really called. Or if they've ever had a name at all. I think it's a recent mutation."

"It's pretty incredible," Paul said, glancing over his shoulder for a better look. His earlier bravado seemed to have vanished, replaced by a surprising air of wonder. Not many people other than Clarke were intrigued by plants.

"What's incredible?" she asked.

Paul shook his head. "Nothing on Earth looks or acts the way they told us it would. The flowers we read about are poisonous. The deer have two heads. The vines have turned carnivorous. And at first, it all seems kind of terrifying and monstrous, but there's a logic to it, you know? All these species, doing what they have to do to survive. They're all fighters. I like that."

Clarke surprised herself by smiling. "You consider yourself a fighter? You seem a little too cheerful for that."

Paul smiled back. It was wistful, almost sad. "Sometimes being cheerful is a way of fighting. When you've seen some of the stuff I've seen . . ." He shook his head. "Let's just say I didn't have the easiest time growing up." Clarke stared at him, wondering if perhaps Paul and Bellamy had more in common than anyone imagined. They'd both had tough childhoods but had chosen different ways of coping: Bellamy turned distant and rebellious, believing there was no one he could trust but himself, while Paul had tried to be open and amiable, someone other people could trust.

Paul shrugged. "But hey, who did, right? I assume it wasn't all rainbows for you, or else you wouldn't have ended up in Confinement."

Clarke blanched slightly, thinking of Lily and the other kids she'd been unable to save. "It's . . . complicated."

He smiled at her—a kind, sincere smile, a world away from his usual overly cheery grin. "I doubt that," he said quietly. "I'm sure you were just trying to do the right thing."

They walked until it got dark, and then continued well into the night. Bellamy was right. It made sense to cover as much ground as possible at night, when they'd be harder to spot, and then rest for brief periods when they got tired. He was clearly having no trouble tracking the enemy. Every so often, he'd return to the group to point out a wagon rut Clarke never would've noticed in broad daylight, let alone at night. The longer they walked, the more energy Bellamy seemed to gain. He was practically bouncing now, eager to keep going and find the men who'd taken his sister.

But everyone else was growing weary, and eventually Bellamy conceded that they should rest for a bit. He hurried ahead to scout a good spot, and about half an hour later, the others caught up to him in a valley at the bottom of a hill, next to a little creek.

Though the evening was chilly, they all agreed not to build a fire, lest the smoke attract unwanted attention. The people who'd brought blankets laid them out on the ground. Clarke watched in fascination as Cooper and Vale half buried themselves under mounds of dried leaves.

"Do you want to give that a shot?" a quiet voice asked. She turned to see Bellamy grinning at her.

Seeing him smile filled her chest with warmth, as the worry weighing her down drained away. "I don't need to. I brought a blanket, unlike some very noble, very foolish people I know."

Bellamy crossed his arms and gave an exaggerated shiver. "What do you think, Doc?" he asked, craning his head back to look at the sky. "Will I risk exposure? Frostbite?"

"Don't worry. If you get frostbite, I'm sure I'll be able to amputate without much trouble. That knife you brought is pretty sharp, right?"

"Of course, there is always preventative medicine."

"Yeah," Clarke said, elbowing him in the side. "Like bringing a *blanket*."

"I did bring one."

"What are you talking about? I saw you take it out of your pack."

Bellamy smiled, and without another word, scooped Clarke off the ground, walked a little bit away from the others, and then toppled them both over into a massive pile of dried leaves.

"Let me go!" Clarke said with a laugh, scrambling to sit up.

"Man, this is one feisty blanket," Bellamy said, wrapping his arms around her waist and pulling her back down toward him.

Her fatigue caught up with her, settling into her limbs. She relaxed and allowed herself to sink into him, resting her head on his chest. "Now this is what the doctor ordered," Bellamy said quietly, running his hand through her hair.

"Leave the medicine to me, Blake," she said sleepily. She took a deep breath, smiling as her senses flooded with her favorite scent in the world, a mix of campfire smoke, damp earth, pine needles, and salt: the smell of Bellamy.

He kissed the top of her head. "Get some rest."

She snuggled deeper against him. "You too." But instead of feeling his breathing grow steady and his arms relax as he drifted off with her, she could tell he was wide-awake, his heart racing.

Clarke lifted her head. Bellamy's eyes were open, his jaw tense.

"It's going to be okay. We'll find them and bring them home."

"Just go to sleep, Clarke."

"You need to sleep too. We need you rested."

"I can't sleep." A slight edge had crept into his voice.

"Bellamy . . ." She traced his cheek with her fingers. "You have to try—"

He wrenched his head to the side, and she let her hand fall. Clarke sat up. "I'm worried about them too, you know. Wells is my best friend, and I love Octavia and Eric and—"

He closed his eyes and winced, as if her words were causing him physical pain. "Just stop, okay? You can't understand. You've never had a sibling, you don't know what it's like. And now I've lost two." When he opened his eyes again, the tenderness from moments earlier was gone, replaced by a fierceness that made her want to lean away. "But they'll pay. There won't be any of those bald bastards left when I'm through with them."

Clarke stared at him, startled. "Bellamy, we're not planning a *battle*. We're going to sneak in and get our people out. Or maybe even negotiate with their captors. There could be a peaceful solution."

"A *peaceful solution*?" Bellamy spat. "Are you kidding me?"

"We only have two guns, and we have no idea what kind

of forces we're facing. We can't turn this into a suicide mission just because you're in the mood to shoot something."

Bellamy stood up so quickly, Clarke was nearly knocked backward. "You still don't trust me, do you? You think I'm just some hotheaded idiot without enough brain cells to come up with a coherent plan."

Clarke sighed. "No, of course that's not it. I just think there's a possibility that—"

"You're never going to trust me, will you? I'll always be the Waldenite delinquent who messes everything up." He stared at her as if seeing her for the first time.

"That's not true!" Clarke rushed forward to place her hand on his arm, but he jerked away.

"Go to sleep," he said curtly. "We need to start moving again in a few hours."

"Bellamy, wait . . ."

But he'd already disappeared into the shadows.

CHAPTER *12*

Glass

Glass and the seven other girls seized from the camp stood in a long row. In their newly issued white dresses, they looked like the spokes of the picket fence Luke had built around their cabin.

They'd been led from the den through a series of winding, crumbling hallways into a vast, empty hall. Huge chunks of the ceiling and walls were missing, and early-morning sunlight pooled on the floor. A few flowering trees grew out of the cracks in the cement, filling the air with a subtle, sweet fragrance. In another situation, it might've seemed pretty, or at least striking, but the longer Glass spent at the Stone, the more her stomach filled with dread.

She wasn't sure what was going on here, but it all felt very, very wrong.

"What are they going to do to us?" Octavia whispered to her.

"I don't know," Glass said, glancing around nervously.

A blond woman in her late twenties, wearing a gray tunic dress, walked up and down the line, inspecting the girls. With each tiny frown or eyebrow raise, Glass grew more anxious. She didn't know what they were being evaluated on, and even worse, she didn't know whether it was better to fail or succeed.

The woman in gray reached Glass, looked her up and down, then peered into Glass's eyes, unblinking. Glass wasn't sure what to do except stare back. But it felt so intrusive, so personal, she could only hold the woman's gaze for a second before averting her eyes.

The woman had already moved on to Octavia before Glass had a chance to gauge her reaction, beyond a vague sense that it had not gone well. But should she be upset or relieved? What was the point of impressing these people?

Survival, came the answer. It was like she was on autopilot, feeling nothing but a stark determination to do whatever it took to get out of here. To get back to the camp. To get back to Luke.

When the line of girls started to move, it took a glance

of warning from Octavia for Glass to realize she needed to follow.

"We're going on a tour of the Stone before your cleansing," the blond woman called out. "Soren wishes for you to get a feel for your new home, now that you're staying with us."

"*Staying* with them?" Lina whispered from behind Glass. "They make it sound like we're guests."

Glass nodded, but said nothing, not wanting to incur the wrath of the woman who was already watching them suspiciously.

"This is the scullery," the woman called from the front of the line, as they wound their way down a corridor.

They passed a bombed-out, windowless space, and Glass got a view of a few red-faced women in white dresses scrubbing earthenware on one side and clothing on the other side in giant, steaming pots. Something to look forward to.

The woman stopped, hand raised, and nodded into the room. "Tomorrow, all of you will take a turn with each of our tasks and will be given a position based on aptitude."

Octavia scoffed quietly beside Glass. "Right. *Aptitude.* To see whether we have a god-given gift for washing disgusting clothes, or an innate talent for cleaning dishes."

The woman in gray scowled at Octavia, and she fell silent.

The line moved again, and soon they were being led outside. In the distance, Glass saw a group of Protectors with shaved heads running alongside some exhausted-looking figures. From the way the Protectors were screaming at them, Glass gathered that they were also prisoners. Were more of her friends among them? She squinted into the sunlight, mind racing.

More alert than she'd been before, Glass tried to observe as many details as she could about the Stone. What had looked like a single structure from the outside was more like a collection of buildings in a honeycomb pattern, not unlike the layout of the Colony. Some structures they passed were no more than skeletons, bare steel beams surrounding piles of rubble, while others were more intact.

White-clad Protectors were everywhere, but oddly, they didn't seem to be doing much. Since she'd arrived at the Colonists' camp, every day was a constant flurry of activity, with people weeding the garden, collecting firewood, chasing after the children, or building new structures. What did these people *do* all day?

There were at least some signs of actual life in the center of the building, which the woman called the "Heart of the Stone" as she led them toward it. It was a tiny forest—maybe a courtyard once—now full of trees, some of them bearing fruit. Glass breathed in the smell of ripening apples and pears, dimly hearing the woman's droning explanation of something about religious ceremonies and offerings to Earth. The group started out again before Glass was ready to leave the comforting green canopy.

"Now I will take you all to meet our leader and see our bounty," the blond woman said reverentially, leading them back through the building. "Soren has returned from a long spirit walk and is eager to meet you all." Glass and Lina exchanged nervous glances. *Meet* felt like an odd word to use with girls who'd been drugged and kidnapped. And this was the person in charge, who'd given the orders and approved the Protectors' violent actions.

The building opened up onto a huge vista, so sprawling and bright that Glass nearly staggered from the scope of it. An enormous rectangular field full of planters stretched out before them, and beyond that, a river basin, glittering in the midday sunshine. As her eyes adjusted, she took in more details: the remains of fallen buildings along the far horizon, the crops in the field. There was a lone woman in a white dress picking through the crops with a careful squint, her black hair falling over one shoulder.

Something strange caught her eye, and Glass stepped closer to get a better glimpse. There were *wheels* under-neath one of the planters, this one full of potatoes and other root vegetables. As the blond woman started a speech about Earth's bounty, two realizations struck Glass: that potatoes grew under the ground, not in heaped piles, and that every single planter here had wheels.

They weren't planters at all. They were carts. This wasn't a farm, just a place to sort through the food these people had looted.

Anger swept aside her fear as Glass thought about how hard everyone had worked getting ready for the Harvest Feast. The weeks spent working the fields, the hours spent hunting, the days spent gathering and drying fruit.

"You're just *thieves*." The words tumbled out of Glass's mouth before she had time to stop them. Next to her, Lina gasped and shook her head, but it was too late.

The woman stopped talking, eyes narrowing, as everyone turned to stare. "How *dare* you speak about the Protectors that way." Glass recoiled as the woman strode toward her, hand raised.

But then the dark-haired woman from the field strolled up, wiping dirty hands on her white tunic dress. The blond woman stopped in her tracks.

"Peace, sister," the dark-haired woman said. "I'd like to hear what she has to say." Her eyes were crinkled at the corners, and bright with curiosity. She smiled at Glass, and there was only warmth in it.

"Please, tell me," the woman said. "How are we thieves?"

An alarm rang in Glass's mind, warning her to be careful despite the woman's gentle demeanor. But then she thought about the anguish in Luke's face when he saw her dragged away. The terrified screams and shouts of pain that filled the clearing after the explosions went off.

"This *bounty* isn't some gift from the Earth. It's food you stole from communities who worked hard to feed their people, their children. You have a field here," Glass said, motioning to it. "Why aren't you growing anything? Do you people not know how?"

The older woman nodded earnestly. "We *do* know how, actually. But Earth has not yet given permission. We can't disrupt the soil for our own selfish needs until we find the place where we'll plant our civilization's roots. Earth must first send us a sign. Then and only then will we evolve from foragers to farmers."

"How big a sign do you need?" Glass asked, feeling as though she was walking a dangerous line. "You've got an enormous fortress. A perfect space for planting. You've even got fruit trees growing in the middle of the grounds— the Heart, you call it? You could easily turn that into an orchard. Then you wouldn't need to attack innocent people and steal their food."

The dark-haired woman was reaching out for Glass's

hands. Confused, Glass let her take them, and the woman pressed them between her own rough palms.

"I appreciate your passion," the woman said, looking into Glass's eyes. As she released Glass's hands and backed away, she nodded to the woman in gray and pointed to Glass, some kind of signal that made Glass's stomach twist. Then she turned to the rest of the group. "Greetings, new friends. It is *such* a pleasure to meet you all. My name is Soren."

A cloud drifted past the sun, rearranging the scenery as Glass's mind scrambled to make new sense of everything surrounding her. *She* was Soren. Their leader.

"I go by a number of names here," Soren went on, reaching up to tie her gray-streaked dark hair into a bun at the nape of her neck. "Some call me High Protector, others prefer Mother Protector, or Mother, for short. Most people just call me Soren, though, which is my real name, and that's fine too!" She laughed, a refreshingly normal sound after all the strange rituals and chanting. "I'm not fussy about titles. The important thing is that you know what my purpose is, and that's twofold: helping you find a home here, and serving Earth with all of my soul."

Soren closed her eyes for a long moment. When the older woman's eyes opened, they looked even brighter and more peaceful than before.

"We'll have time to get to know each other as we go about our work," she said, greeting each girl in the line with a smile. "But today, I'd like to leave you with a few thoughts about *mothers*. I consider myself the mother of everyone here." She stopped in front of Lina, and smoothed her glossy hair. "You included."

To Glass's surprise, Lina blushed and looked at her feet.

"Mothers are wise," Soren went on. "They care for others, and giving this gift gives *them* one in return—they're connected to the soil, to the air, to their intuition in a way that's special and important." She laced her fingers together, pivoting to face the others. "Mothers are also strong. They don't bend to their children's whims. They *instruct*. They shape them into the best people they can be."

Soren's eyes met Glass's, but this time, Glass didn't look away. She couldn't wrap her mind around the disconnect between Soren's warmth and the Protectors' violence. She'd seen them attack her camp. She'd watched them almost kill Luke. Yet standing here, listening to Soren's calm words, she felt her anger begin to melt away.

"What I want you to take away, as you get to know our little enclave here and the things we're hoping to accomplish, is that we women must be *mothers* to our people." Soren grinned. "Especially the men. They're children, really! All humans are. They're innocent, but dangerously reckless in that innocence. They're takers. We need to show them the way. What has been done to Earth—the greatest mother of all—is nothing short of heartbreaking. Even before the Shattering, this world was overrun with spoiled *children* and their toys, poisoning the air and the waters, building and harvesting and chopping to suit their own needs. There were gods, religions, but the highest power of all was selfishness."

Soren's brow furrowed, and she took a deep breath. "We've been given another chance. To do better. To be better. And I'll need your help to make it happen. You, the *women* among us."

Soren pressed her hands to her heart, and to her surprise, Glass felt something stirring inside her own chest. She'd tried so hard to make herself useful these last few weeks, but there never seemed to be a place for her back at camp. She didn't know how to heal the sick or design buildings. She couldn't carry heavy loads of firewood. She could never come up with fun games to amuse the children. But maybe Soren was right. Perhaps there *was* a role for Glass on Earth, one that she could do well, without letting people down.

"We all serve Earth, and if you serve Her well, one day you may stand where I do, as the highest Protector of all . . . if Earth wills it." Soren beamed. "That's a little custom of ours. When one of us says, 'If Earth wills it,' we all repeat it, to sort of encourage it along. Shall we give it a try? *If Earth wills it . . .*"

And everyone hesitantly repeated, "If Earth wills it."

"A good start," Soren said, clapping. "Welcome to our family."

CHAPTER *13*

Wells

Wells took another step into the river, the cold water stinging his bare stomach. He gritted his teeth, dug his toes into the slippery mud, and kept going.

Next to him, Eric shivered, teeth chattering. On the other side, Kit, the Earthborn who'd been taken with them, walked into the water with a placid expression. Maybe he was more used to the frigid temperatures than the climate-controlled Colonists were. Down the line, Graham clenched his jaw as the river water splashed over his torso.

"You may stop there." A musical voice rang out from the riverbank, and all the prisoners turned to face the compound. A row of armed, white-uniformed Protectors waited on the bank to ensure the prisoners' cooperation in this "voluntary" ceremony. Behind them, the High Protector, Soren, stood on a stacked pile of rubble, gazing out like a benevolent goddess.

Soren had visited the barracks this morning, and Wells had been a little surprised to see a woman leading these brutal, violent people. It turned out all the key decision-makers here were female. The men were just the muscle who carried out their orders. When Soren had spoken to the "newest of our flock," as she'd called the prisoners, she'd told them all about a ceremony they would partici-pate in to cleanse them of their past transgressions. She'd seemed so reasonable, and the way she'd described this ceremony had sounded more benign than the reality of it; all the boys were shuddering in the frigid water, struggling to stay upright in the river's rushing current.

Wells waited for Soren to issue the next set of instruc-tions, but instead, maddeningly, she turned and motioned behind her, ushering another group of prisoners to the water's edge.

This group was all female. Wells inhaled sharply, frantically scanning them. He remembered what the Protectors had said on the wagon about keeping "the best of your women," but since he hadn't yet laid eyes on them, he hadn't dared picture who might have been taken.

There they were, shivering in identical sleeveless white shifts. Eight of the girls from the camp. His heart sank when he saw Lina and Octavia, and pain jolted through his chest when his eyes landed on Glass. His childhood friend had endured so much suffering already, and now here she was, facing what could be the most dangerous challenge yet. Luke must've been out of his mind with worry right now. Bellamy too. The girls looked unharmed, thank god. But knowing they were here, among these monsters, sent waves of pain through his chest.

Wells took a deep breath and willed his rage to subside. He would make sure his friends made it home. And if it turned out the Protectors had hurt anyone back at the camp, then Wells would make them suffer for it. But this was not the moment.

Glass caught Wells's eye and stared at him in astonishment. He could read her face like a book. She was dismayed that he'd also been captured, but relieved that he was there with her. Afraid that it would all go terribly wrong.

The girls waded into the water with sharp intakes of breath. Wells tried to catch Octavia's eye, but she didn't turn, just stared ahead, her mouth set in a defiant grimace as she swished her arms in the river's waves.

"You may stop there," Soren said again, spreading her arms wide while the girls stopped a few yards ahead of

Wells and turned to face her. "Welcome, new friends. It is such a blessing to have you all with us."

Her voice was warm, and her expression kind. But Wells refused to let those details distract him from the fact that there was something seriously wrong with these people.

"Earth has wrought Her incredible work and brought you into our fold. You were raised in different communities than ours, under different customs." She cast her eyes upward as if amused. "Some of you, as I understand it, have even come to us from the sky. We honor your backgrounds. But now it is time to wash them away and start again, as clean as the moment of your birth. When I release my arms," Soren said, still holding them wide, "I would like you to submerge your heads under the water and rise again, anew."

Her arms dropped. As commanded, Wells ducked under the icy shock of water. He opened his eyes, surprised by the sight of a fluorescent fish swimming by, then stood straight with a gasp, letting the river slough back off him.

"As your body is now cleaned, I ask you to wipe your minds clear as well," Soren said, her gaze traveling over all of them. "Not of your education or your skills. Those are gifts from Earth Herself. Clear your mind instead of assumptions. Get rid of what you have always clung to as truth. Walk among us open-minded. Be a vessel into which

Earth can pour Her wisdom, and you will be well on your way to serving as a true Protector, and a friend to this great community—the last and *only* empire, if Earth wills it."

"If Earth wills it," Wells repeated, along with everybody else. The more he looked like he was buying into this nonsense, the easier it'd be to earn their trust . . . and then use it against them.

"And now," Soren said brightly, "we celebrate!" She smiled and motioned them out of the water, the young women first, and then the men.

Wells rubbed drips of water from his eyes until he could spot the gathering in the distance. There was a large grassy rectangular field just past the river's edge lined with tables full of food and drink. As Wells waded out of the river, a small woman in a white dress offered him a cloth to dry himself.

"Thank you," he said. She blinked in reply and scurried off.

Wells strolled through the gathering, peering down at the baskets piled with food, wondering which of it was plundered from his own camp. That bushel of bruised apples? The sweet potatoes? The rolls, made with someone else's grains? Wells took one of each and wandered away from the tables, looking for Graham and Eric.

Wells found his gaze drawn back to the riverbank, where two girls were lingering, heads bent close as they talked. The blond one glanced nervously over her shoulder—it was Glass and Octavia. Whatever they were discussing, they weren't being half as covert as they thought they were. The women in gray were watching them from the field.

Glass caught his eye and started to mouth something to him, but he shook his head. Instead, he smiled back dimly, using that same placid expression he saw on all the Protectors, then motioned for Glass and Octavia to join him.

He found a spot on a blanket near the compound walls and settled in with his food. A few minutes later, Glass and Octavia made their way over and sat down beside him. Wells had to force himself not to glare at the Protectors who watched their movements with appraising eyes.

"Are you all right?" Glass asked, leaning over to give him a quick hug.

"I'm fine," he said. "Keep smiling."

She did.

Octavia smiled too, but hers wasn't half as convincing. "We're leaving," Octavia said through gritted teeth. "I saw some boats tied up by the river. Whenever we get the opportunity, we're going to make a run for them."

Wells could feel his pulse jump in his wrists, his stomach, his throat. He kept smiling. "When?"

Octavia's fake smile vanished as she pressed her lips together into a determined line. "As soon as possible. Tonight maybe."

"Hold on," Wells whispered before craning his head to nod respectfully at a blond woman in a gray dress passing silently by. Once she was out of earshot, he took a bite of his apple, stretching his legs casually in front of him. "Whatever you're thinking of doing, don't do it. Not yet."

Octavia's eyes narrowed. "Why not?"

Glass answered for him. "It isn't the right time yet."

"Exactly," Wells said, offering her a bite of apple. Glass shook her head politely and glanced away.

"Seems like a perfect time to me," Octavia said, reaching out to claim the bite Glass had passed on. "There are boats tied up on the water *right now*. We can—"

"We can *what*?" Wells whispered quickly. The field was filling up fast and their window for chatting was closing. "Row away while they shoot at us?"

Octavia frowned, but he saw her considering.

"It could be the start of a plan," he said patiently. "But we've got no weapons, no help, and they don't trust us enough to let their guard down yet. Even if we were to get away, all the way back home, they'd just march straight back there and do the same thing they did before—only worse this time."

"What are you thinking?" Glass asked quietly, pinching off a corner of the stale loaf of bread and rolling it between her finger and thumb.

"We'll become Protectors," Wells said. "All of us. Graham, Eric, Kit, and the other guys from our camp are on board. Talk to the other girls who were captured and spread the word. We do whatever it takes to make them trust us, to believe that we want to join them. Then, once they trust us and let their guard down, we're out of here. That way, when we escape, it'll be with our own weapons in our hands and a fighting chance of making it home."

Octavia went quiet, and for a moment, Wells worried that she was going to argue with him, loudly, right here, surrounded by their enemies. Then she slowly nodded and peered up at him.

"The long game . . . okay, I'm with you, Jaha."

Wells smiled, then glanced over at Glass, expecting to see her nodding in agreement. But she was staring into the distance, a strange expression on her face, one that, for the first time in their long friendship, he couldn't quite read. He wondered if she was thinking about Luke . . . but no, it wasn't that. There was no element of pain, just wistfulness.

"Glass? You on board with the plan?" Wells asked.

At the sound of her name, she startled and turned to him. "What? Yes, of course."

A hint of something he did recognize flashed across her face. After so many years, and so many secrets, he could always tell when she was lying.

CHAPTER 14

Bellamy

Crouched behind a mossy jumble of rotting branches, Bellamy watched the sun set over the largest building he'd ever seen.

This had to be the place. And this was definitely the moment. It'd taken them far too long to get here. Over the past day of hiking, the terrain had grown choppy and treacherous, the ruins of a fallen cityscape littered the forest with hidden hazards, hills and crests and sheer drop-offs were in every direction. But finally they were here, and there wasn't a second to waste. Every second they waited was one during which something terrible could happen to Octavia, Wells, and the rest of their friends.

A pack of men in white had filed out of the building a few minutes ago, wagons rolling behind them. The sight of them had released a torrent of bubbling rage, and it'd taken all his self-control not to lunge at them. There hadn't been any movement since then—on anybody's part.

"Let's go for it," Bellamy whispered to the others.

"The sun's setting," Clarke said tentatively. "Maybe we should fall back and make camp somewhere we can establish a perimeter." She looked away while she spoke, as if afraid of setting Bellamy off.

"Good plan, Griffin," Paul said, nodding emphatically. "We'll be better off under the cover of darkness."

And what would you know about that? Bellamy wanted to ask. *You were an "officer" on a space station where there was no night . . . and no real enemies.* But then he saw most of the others nodding as well and sighed inwardly. There was no way he could storm this concrete fortress on his own. He needed the others with him, and if they wanted to fall back, then that was the way it had to be. For now.

As Bellamy stood up and started to stretch, cracking his back with a quiet groan, Paul turned back and called, "One of us should stay here and keep watch. Bellamy?" There was a challenge in his eyes.

"I'll do it," Felix said, breaking the tension. "Just send someone back to tell me where you're camped so I can get word to you if anything changes."

Paul looked disappointed, but he nodded, then turned to the rest of the group, saying, "Keep low and *stay quiet*," in the loudest whisper Bellamy had ever heard.

They started away silently, a single winding line through the woods, following the same track they'd taken in. Clarke lingered in the back with Bellamy. "Are you okay with that plan? I think it'll give us the best shot."

"Yes. Fine," he said, not meeting her eyes. They'd barely exchanged more than a few words since last night. He felt as if he was being torn in half. Part of him wanted to pull her into his arms and beg her to forgive him for acting like an ass. But an equally strong part of him wasn't ready to forgive *her*. What did he have to do to make her trust him?

"Hey, Clarke," Paul called. "Come look at this crazy bug . . . wait, hold on . . . no way! I think it's a frog with *wings*. It's got the strangest face."

Without another word to Bellamy, Clarke jogged up to where Paul was standing at the edge of a small pond. Bellamy scowled at Paul's back.

The group continued walking, and Bellamy followed them around the bend of a little tributary, covering their tracks as he went. Finally, Clarke motioned to the shell of an old building. Some of its steel beams were still intact, dripping with moss so thick it formed a funny kind of wall on two sides, thick enough to shield them from view from a distance.

"This should work fine," Paul said, his hand reaching out to rest on Clarke's shoulder. "Good eye, Griffin."

"A fire's going to be too conspicuous," Clarke said, turning away. Paul's hand dropped off her. "We'll have to do our best without one."

Touch her one more time, and your face will be indistinguishable from the frog's, Bellamy thought, balling his fists. He forced himself to breathe, then set to work constructing a circle of makeshift trip alarms around the camp. When he returned to the center, he saw Clarke sitting cross-legged on the ground, drawing a diagram of the raiders' massive fortress in the dirt with a stick. Paul leaned over her, one hand on her shoulder—*again*—as if for balance. And she wasn't shooing him off. She wasn't doing anything.

Bellamy couldn't watch this for a second longer. Instead, he turned and started away.

"Hey!" Clarke called from behind him. "Where are you going?"

"To tell Felix where we are," Bellamy said, glancing over his shoulder.

She frowned, looking down again.

"Good man," Paul said cheerfully, pointing at him.

Bellamy didn't bother to reply. He trekked back through the woods, trying to untangle the jealousy that was eating him up inside. But all it did was make him more restless, more eager for action. The arrows on his back felt heavy in their leather quiver.

At the sound of footsteps, Felix spun around quickly. But when he realized it was just Bellamy, he relaxed and raised a hand in greeting. "You're back. Great. So where are you guys camped?"

"Doesn't matter," Bellamy said without stopping. He motioned for Felix to follow him. "We're going this way."

Felix glanced over his shoulder. "What about the others? Where are we going?"

"Scouting mission. You coming?"

He hesitated for a second, then nodded. "Definitely."

Bellamy scanned the ivy-covered fortress ahead, looming above them like a monster in the night. There was no one coming or going at the moment. He darted ahead from post to post, Felix doing the same a few yards away.

He took in as many details as he could. A wide, rocky courtyard with wheel ruts cut in the middle for a cart track. A low doorway cut into a solid wall, likely heavily guarded. Subtle gun turret points scattered along the top of the high wall in every direction, none of them manned right now, by the looks of it.

These people weren't exactly on high alert. And why would they be? They'd wiped out their competition, practically scorched them from the face of the Earth, and taken all their weapons too.

Bellamy ran his hand down his carved bow, then darted ahead again, this time to the side of the building, if you could even call it that. This structure was impossibly vast, bigger than the three ships of the Colony combined. Bellamy felt his stomach sinking at the thought of a group of people populous enough to fill it. How could he possibly hope to bring a society like that to its knees?

But then he stopped, crouching in the tall, reedy grass, and listened the way he listened to the forest back home. He could hear a low buzz of sound from inside the fortress, but something deeper than his normal senses told him that this building wasn't full at all.

This could be why they took our people, he realized with a cold chill. *Maybe they raid in order to bolster their ranks.* That would be a pretty piss-poor strategy. Kill your prisoners' friends and family and then expect them to join you in happily marauding even more people?

The moon emerged from behind a curtain of clouds, and in the sudden glow, Bellamy could make out more about the structure of the building. What had looked like a solid, impregnable wall covered in climbing plants was actually perforated by small windows, their glass long-since blown out. That was a danger for anyone approaching, plenty of spots for rifles to poke through. But could it also be an opportunity?

He crept up to one of the windows and glanced through it. On the other side was some sort of indoor path or road. It may have been a hallway once upon a time, but now the moonlight was illuminating the pathway; the ceiling had caved in all the way around. Bellamy realized that the outer wall was just that: a protective wall, unconnected to the rest of the structure. Maybe if they could find some way to get beyond this wall, they could get their people back.

Felix sprinted ahead, pointing to the flash of light along the horizon to the right. Bellamy peered toward him and spotted it too: a wide river running alongside the building, a smaller lagoon spilling from it practically all the way to the walls themselves. The only thing between the rippling water and the building was a large, terraced, rectangular green field, somewhat less unkempt than the other surrounding spaces, along with a riverside "beach" so rocky that Bellamy suspected it was probably once used as a road.

He wanted to keep going, get a closer look, but the way there was jagged with dunes of debris; it would be hard to pick their way out if they ran into trouble. Felix was already racing away, though, no doubt thinking about Eric, held prisoner somewhere nearby. His back was turned and he was too far to hear a whistle of warning, so Bellamy followed, darting from dune to dune.

Then he spotted movement in the field ahead of them. He froze, watching as five figures emerged from the fortress, none of them a soldier with a shaved head. They were all women, most draped in rippling gray fabric. The one in the front was an older woman in white with long dark hair, her hands raised toward the hazy outline of the moon.

Shivers ran down Bellamy's spine at the sight of them. There was something overly deliberate about the way they were walking, like the raiders during the attack, timing each step down to the precise measurement. And they were humming, making low, guttural noises, like bees emerging from a hive. Bellamy didn't know what was going on here, but he didn't like it.

The woman in front crouched down to touch the grass and the others followed suit, pressing their fingers to their mouths when they finished, then up to the sky.

"Great Earth," the woman called out. "We have carried out Your wishes and will do so for the rest of our days.

Now we humbly entreat You for a sign. Is this our home? Is this where we shall remain? Our stone, our hearth, our keep?"

Behind him, Bellamy could hear the wind traveling through the forest in a nearly imperceptible whisper. The woman on the lawn cocked her head. She heard it too.

"If you wish us to remain, Great Earth, send Your wind to embrace us," she called out. Bellamy barely had time to blink before the wind reached him, whipping his hair into a mop, continuing on to rustle the skirts of the ladies on the lawn, all of whom looked amazed and exultant.

Except the dark-haired one, of course.

What a bullshit artist, Bellamy thought. *If there hadn't been any wind, she would have ordered the air to keep still.*

"We have our answer, friends," she said, a little lower, then turned, arms raised, to herd them back inside. But just before she'd turned completely around, she stopped, still as a statue.

Bellamy held his breath. Her eyes scanned over the rubble-strewn valley, straight past him and away.

"Let's rest," she said pleasantly, her shoulders relaxing, then disappeared back into the wall with the others.

After a careful moment, Felix crossed over the debris to huddle beside Bellamy. "What the hell was that?" he whispered.

"Someone to look out for," Bellamy whispered back. "I think we've pressed our luck enough for one day."

"Yeah," Felix said, already starting away. "Agreed. Let's head b—"

The ground roared as the rocks gave way beneath Felix's feet, swallowing him up in one clattering gulp. Jaw agape, Bellamy scrambled on his hands and knees, peering into the spot his friend had vanished into.

Then he let out a breath, panic giving way to relief.

Felix was crumpled, confused but uninjured, on the floor of what looked like a cellar. He peered up at Bellamy sheepishly. "Looks like I found a way in?"

Without a moment of hesitation, Bellamy slid his legs into the opening and dropped silently down beside Felix. He looked around, seeing a dim light in the distance. This had been a tunnel once, then.

He pulled the little makeshift dagger he'd carved from rock out of his pocket and positioned it in his hand, in case of trouble. Then he nodded forward, toward the light. "Let's go."

Felix followed in a fast crouch, their footsteps echoing lightly in the cavernous space despite their best attempts to keep quiet. This was reckless, this was foolish . . . and this was by far the best shot they'd gotten yet.

Bellamy's step slowed. Something was blocking the way

ahead—a cart, maybe, loaded with something he couldn't identify. He listened for the sound of raiders, but made out nothing. With a nod to Felix, he continued, reaching his hands out for the edge of the wagon so he could push it clear enough to give them space to edge past.

Then his hand grazed the top of the wood, coming away with one of the objects inside. It was round, ridged, with a little metal pin on top. Bellamy's breath turned to ice in his throat. He put it back, carefully, and let his fingers travel lightly along the rest. Then he backed up a step, wonderstruck.

"Holy. Shit." He let out a silent laugh. "This cart is full of weapons. There are guns, bombs . . . just what we need."

Felix shook his head, peering past Bellamy to check for himself. "You have got to be kidding me."

Bellamy smiled. "If this is a joke, it's on them. They're probably guarding the inner door to this hallway. They think it's a dead end. And it *will* be, soon enough."

"What's your plan?" Felix asked eagerly.

Bellamy lifted one of the grenades up so that he could see it in the light. "We're going to stick these in every little window we can find. We're going to blow down these god-damned walls, walk right into the middle of the fortress, and take back everything and everyone that was stolen from us."

A smile spread across Felix's face. "You want to *raid* them, you mean."

"They did it to us," Bellamy said, carefully pocketing the grenade as he turned to go, a new fire igniting his step. "It's time we returned the favor."

CHAPTER 15

Glass

Glass woke up gasping. Someone was shaking her shoulder with a cruel, cold grip.

The blond Protector peered down at her, her hair tied back in a tight bun. Glass's mind reached for the woman's name as her eyes adjusted to the dark, making out her severely beautiful features. *Margot*, Glass remembered. *One of Soren's advisors.*

And at that realization, her heart clenched, her mind spooling back to that moment on the field when Soren had pointed to Glass. It must've been an order to Margot. The High Protector hadn't approved of her little speech, and now Glass was going to find out what the consequences were.

Margot started dragging her upward by the armpit. Glass fought against her. "No, no, whatever I've done, I swear I'll be better! I'll keep my mouth shut, I'll—"

"Shhh, you'll wake the others," Margot hissed. "Don't be selfish, they need their rest for the workday ahead."

It was such a mundane thing to say that Glass fell silent, more from confusion now than fear.

"I don't know what she sees in you," Margot whispered as Glass stood beside her. "But I trust you'll prove yourself useful in time."

Margot led her silently out of the room, tiptoeing around the sleeping forms of the other girls, some with their feet still stubbornly dangling off the side of the cots so their toes could touch the ground. Those were the true believers, Glass knew. She kept well clear of them.

Glass passed Anna's cot and nearly jostled it with her foot to rouse her. It seemed like a good idea to have somebody witness her being led out of the dorms in the dark of night, but she didn't want to risk alerting Margot.

Once they'd left the dorms, Margot turned back to lock the door. "Where are we going?" Glass dared to whisper.

"To Soren's quarters," Margot answered. "Mother keeps odd hours, so you'd best get used to wake-ups like this one."

Glass kept pace, her brain catching up. She still found

it disorienting how the Protectors called Soren "mother." Were any of them really her children?

They turned left, continuing down the endless, roofless hall. Glass looked up at the stars winking in the pre-dawn light and wondered where Luke was. Was he awake, exhausted and distraught, staring at the same stars as he crafted a plan to come rescue her? She wished there was a way to send him a message, to let him know that she was fine.

Margot stopped, motioning Glass up a wooden stair-way that still smelled like sawdust. As she climbed up the stairs, Glass felt Margot's hand on her shoulder. She winced, expecting an impatient shove. But, to her surprise, the touch was gentle.

Two guards in white stood at the top of the stairs, wear-ing their usual eerily blank expressions. Seeing Glass, they nodded—almost deferentially—and parted to let her pass.

Glass forced a smile over her shoulder and continued on with Margot, both of them emerging into a wide room. Its scorched cement floors were covered with woven rugs and a four-poster bed sat in the middle. In the corner of the room, a fire burned in a makeshift fireplace, a scrap-metal chimney sending the smoke safely through the ceiling and into the night sky.

Glass marveled for a moment at the beauty of the room, the many little luxuries here, before remembering that all of this was likely stolen. Who had spent hours upon hours weaving the red woolen blanket on Soren's bed? Glass hadn't seen much weaving or wool-spinning going on around here.

Before she could take any more in, Margot shuffled her toward a little antechamber just off the main room. There was a cot here, just like back in the dorms, but also a little washbasin, a warm rug on the floor, even a small cracked mirror on the wall.

Glass stared at herself in it with a ripple of shock. It had been so long since she'd seen her own reflection. She looked so thin, so tired . . . so sad. She reached out and touched the crack, half expecting her face to fade and disappear behind it.

Margot's eyes traveled down to Glass's starchy white nightgown. "You're smaller than Dara. We'll have to take in her dress. In the meantime, you can wear your old uniform."

She tossed Glass's white dress onto the bed. Glass blinked, surprised—she hadn't even noticed Margot bundling up her things back at the dorm.

"Who is Dara?" Glass asked, drawing her arms around herself.

"Soren's former maid," Margot said briskly. "You'll be replacing her." Her eyes sharpened on Glass. "She was a lot like you, actually. Sharp mind. Loud mouth."

Glass couldn't read Margot's smirk, but she felt suspicion swirling in her stomach. "What . . . *happened* to Dara?" She pinched the seams of her nightgown, bracing herself for the answer.

"She has risen," came a voice from behind her.

Glass turned to see Soren standing in the doorway, languid and willowy, a slight smile on her face.

"Risen?" Glass asked carefully. Was that their word for dead?

In answer, Soren stepped back, beckoning another girl into the doorway—a broad-shouldered, dark-skinned girl in her early twenties wearing the gray dress of one of the High Protector's advisors.

"Dara," Margot said warmly, reaching out to squeeze the girl's hands. "*Sister.*"

Dara beamed, then nodded politely to Glass. "Mother is particular," she said. "You must have impressed her."

"That she did." Soren laughed, extending a hand for Glass to take. "And will continue to, I have no doubt."

Glass's head was spinning. "What am I meant to be doing, exactly?"

"Your first responsibility is to take a walk with me,"

Soren said, gliding back into her chamber. "I'd like to see the Stone in the dawn light."

Dara's eyes met Glass's. She mouthed, *shoes, shawl*, while Margot motioned to an open chest of clothing a few feet away. Glass hurried to it, drawing away a set of leather slippers and a thick woolen shawl. Dara nodded, and Glass took them to Soren.

Soren smiled in thanks, then squinted at Glass's outfit. "Take one more for yourself, child, so you don't catch a chill."

Dara was already beside her, offering her a soft white cloak.

"Thank you," Glass whispered, both flattered and confused by all the attention.

The Stone was quiet as dawn rose over it in waves of pink and yellow. Glass and Soren walked in surprisingly comfortable silence. Soren knew every little alleyway and shortcut through the labyrinthine structure, leaving Glass completely disoriented. Finally, Glass smelled something green and thick and heady, and knew exactly where they were heading: the Heart of the Stone.

"This is my favorite spot," Soren said, stepping out of the building and into the sprawling courtyard. She led Glass into the trees, among the orchard. "I come here to think. And to talk."

Soren smiled at Glass in an encouraging way, as if to say that Glass should start this conversation. So she blurted the first question on her mind.

"Why did you pick me as your maid?"

Soren brightened. "Because you ask questions like that. You have an honest heart and a bold mouth. But more than that . . ." She turned away, peering up at the light filtering from between the branches of the trees. "I like the way your mind works."

Glass fought an incredulous laugh. In her entire life, no one but Luke had ever paid her that compliment.

"Some people look at the world and see only what they can take from it. What they can reap, steal, carry away." Soren's smile dropped as her expression grew thoughtful. "That's useful, of course. That's what we value in our raiders. But leaders need something more than that. They need to look around them and see what they can provide for *others*." She motioned around her, her eyes glittering with mirth. "Like a field for planting, for example. Or an orchard."

Glass felt her cheeks growing warm. "I don't know why I said all that."

"You said it because it's true." Soren smiled at her. "Your suggestions were wise, Glass. And, as it turns out, you were right." Her smile widened, her face lit by a sudden ray of pink dawn light. "Earth has spoken to us. She wishes us to remain here. We'll build our hearths for the winter, and when the spring comes"—she squeezed Glass's shoulder and stepped away—"we'll plant."

Glass stared at her, unsure how to respond. Part of her was desperate for the Protectors to leave, to go somewhere far away, where they could never hurt the Colonists or the Earthborns again. She wanted to go home to Luke. But another part of her wasn't ready to leave Soren and the way she made Glass feel when she smiled at her. Useful. Wanted. Valuable.

"We've stopped before, you know," Soren said, her voice dropping low. "When I joined the Protectors as a girl, we lived far to the west. We've stopped twice since then, once for each generation, and now it's time to plant again."

Glass's mind swirled with unasked questions: *What does planting have to do with generations? Where in the west did you live? Why did you join them?* But the question that rose to her mouth was, "Soren, why did you take *us* from our camp? Why not everyone?"

Soren stopped strolling, her hand slowly reaching for a low branch laden with plums. She touched the fruit gently, with just the tips of her fingers. "Earth has Her own rhythms, you'll learn, Glass. It is not just foolish to ignore them; it is a great sin. And on Earth, there are takers and there are Protectors. We must stop the takers from harming Earth any more than they already have, while encouraging potential Protectors to bloom. Look at this plum. It's beautiful. It's alive. Growing and perfect, like all of the new members of our community."

Glass's breath caught, listening to the wonderment in Soren's voice, watching the light dancing over the older woman's face. The High Protector's hair was loose and graying slightly, but there was something so beautiful and relaxed about her, like she was just one of the trees in the forest, swaying with them, reaching toward the dawn's glow.

"Mother!" A young voice broke through the orchard's quiet. Glass turned to see an out-of-breath preteen boy racing to greet Soren. "The men are back from the south. It was a success."

"Earth be good!" Soren kissed the top of the boy's head and he beamed.

"Blessings, Mother," he said, blinking up at her.

"Blessings, Callum," she answered back. Whether Soren was his real mother or not, she certainly played the role well. "I'll be with them in just a moment."

The boy sprinted away to deliver her message, and Soren turned to Glass.

"I'll head straight to the barracks," Soren said, pressing

her hand to Glass's wrist. "You go take some time for your-self. Explore a little and see what ideas pop up."

As Glass watched Soren's graceful figure walking away, another image seemed to take her place: a blond woman staring into the artificially lit mirror on Phoenix, her hair carefully curled and coiled, her gown cut low, her smile brittle, her eyes forever guarded.

What would my mother think of these people? Glass wondered. *And what would Soren think of her?*

Soren would think she was a taker, Glass realized. *And she might have been right.* Glass's mother had loved her daughter, and would've done anything for her, but she'd also spent her life manipulating people to get what she wanted, from extra credits at the Exchange, to endless power rations for their apartment. Glass's skin prickled as she remembered the coy glances her mother directed toward Vice Chancellor Rhodes, and the hungry, possessive looks she received in turn.

Glass peered up at the trees, touching a dangling plum with the tip of one careful finger.

Protector. After everything Soren said, it didn't sound half as ominous anymore.

CHAPTER *16*

Wells

It was their third day at the Stone and their training sessions showed no sign of stopping. But this morning, instead of running around the track just inside of the walls, the Protectors had taken them out into the woods for what they were calling "active" training. At the moment, Wells was high in a tree, squinting into the darkness of the forest as a thickly muscled Protector walked beneath him, carrying a gun.

The wind blew, shaking the tree. Wells clung to the branch and exhaled slowly, silently, not moving. He waited. The Protector marched closer, keeping to the path Wells had dug through the undergrowth, a subtle trap to lure him in. The man kept going, heedless, until he was mere seconds from passing directly underneath. Three . . . two . . .

Wells dropped, landing on the Protector's back, one arm snatching the gun out of the startled man's fingers, the other around his neck, elbow tightening and tightening. The man kicked but Wells held on, teeth gritted, sweat dripping from his forehead.

The thunder of sprinting footsteps made his eyes fly up. Two other Protectors approached—fast. Wells spun his captive around, loosened his grip enough to flip and cock the gun, and trained the weapon on the new arrivals.

"Any closer and I shoot," Wells snarled.

Behind him, a twig cracked. "If that had been loaded, I'd have been quaking in my boots," came an all-too-familiar voice.

Wells dropped the prop gun and turned, letting the Protector in his arms go with an apologetic pat on the back. The man gripped his throat, coughing, but knocked Wells's shoulder in reply, mouthing, *nice job*.

"Come on out, everyone," Oak called. "This training round is finished."

The other novice Protectors picked their way out of their hiding spots in the forest and made their way over. Oak waited until they'd all gathered in a loose circle before pointing to Wells with a smirk.

"You didn't need to mouth off at the end, there," Oak said. "You had a gun. That talks a lot louder than you do. And a silent man is an intimidating man. If you talk, they'll think *they* can talk too. Talk you out of it. Instead of warning them . . ." Oak stooped to pick up the rifle, spinning and cocking it with lightning speed. "Just shoot."

He aimed the barrel at Wells's chest and pulled the trigger. It clicked softly. No ammo. Wells exhaled.

"Other than that, not bad," Oak grumbled. "Not bad at all. Which is more than I can say for the rest of you!" He turned to squint disgustedly at the others, stopping briefly at Kit, the Earthborn boy. "You were stealthy, lad. You and this one"—he nodded to Wells—"you're starting to listen to Earth. And She's talking back. Keep it up and you'll be one of us, if Earth wills it."

"If Earth wills it," they all repeated.

"Now get in line and prepare to run!"

Wells started sprinting away, knowing that Oak would catch up within seconds.

Kit glanced at Wells over his shoulder as he jogged away, blinking twice, their signal that all was going as planned. Kit and Eric had talked to all the other guys from their camp that had been captured, and they were on the same page—everyone would play along and make the Protectors think they were on their side so their captors would let their guards down. Then they would find the perfect time to escape. Wells wasn't sure what the other recruits thought—if they were true believers or equally unwilling captives—but for now he and his friends were only speaking to the people they knew.

Wells blinked back and Kit looked away, just as Oak fell in beside him.

"You're running against Earth's soil," Oak snarled. This was the call and repeat they had to do every time they trained.

"I beg Earth's forgiveness," Wells answered.

"You eat Earth's food."

"I thank Earth for Her bounty."

"Pledge yourself to Earth's service."

Wells's stomach tightened. Here it came—the sucker punch—just like every time the demand was made. They kept saying the recruits weren't ready to pledge themselves to Earth's service, that they weren't allowed. And there was no sense in fighting it, not if they wanted the Protectors to believe they were buying this.

Not yet.

"I pledge myself to Earth's service," Wells said, bracing himself.

The silence that followed felt like a free fall. Wells cocked his head, confused. He'd said it. The whole sentence. And

Oak was still just running beside him, aggression firmly in check.

Wells glanced at Oak. The old man wasn't looking at him, just staring down the forest track back to the barracks. His mouth was still set in a surly line, but there was the faintest glint of a smile in his eyes. Wells was making progress.

When they reached the outer courtyard of the Stone, Wells stopped abruptly, as he'd been trained to do, hands behind his back awaiting next orders.

"Break for lunch," Oak barked. "Be back here in an hour."

"Yes, sir," Wells said. Oak stalked off toward the field and Wells watched him with wonder. For the first time since they'd arrived, he was allowed to be on his own. He wasn't being marched to his meal or being watched by his trainer. He wasn't being watched by anyone at all.

Was this his reward for doing well today? For pledging himself to Earth's service?

Wells glanced around and, seeing no one looking, spat into the dirt, as close to a rebellion as he could muster right now. Something told him the planet didn't care. Then, deciding to press his luck a little further, he went inside the Stone to do a little exploring.

The outer roads were bustling with carts today. Another raiding party must have just come in, this one from the south, wagons full of ceramic pots and bowls, woven rugs, winter vegetables, cured meats, and what looked like blocks of salt. Though he kept his expression schooled, anger burned brightly inside him. Who had the Protectors been stealing from now? Destroying *his* camp wasn't enough for them?

Wells kept going, deeper into the structure, taking in as many details as he could in the limited time he was given. A plume of steam came from a wide inner room. He ducked his head inside to see a laundry facility, clothes being dropped into a vat over a fire, red-cheeked girls stirring it, sweat pooling in dark puddles on the backs of their white dresses. He scanned the room, but none of the faces were familiar.

The buzz of furtive whispers drew his attention down the road. The way was blocked by a wall of white fabric dangling from a line that stretched from building to building. He could see two figures outlined behind one sheet by the afternoon sun, their heads close together.

The two figures stepped back, and one of their heads poked out from between the pinned sheets. Wells caught a flash of black hair and red ribbon, glanced behind him for onlookers, and hurried over.

"Octavia," he said, pulling the sheet back, blinded for a second by the sudden flash of sun.

He heard a gasp, then felt something jagged pressing painfully into his neck.

"Wells . . . oh god, I'm sorry." The object drew away and Wells peered down at a startled Octavia. She winced in apology, pocketing the metal scrap she'd been wielding. "I thought you were one of them."

"And what if I *had* been, O?" Wells whispered. "You would have been caught, just like that."

"I don't care." She raised her chin, and for a moment, she looked so much like Bellamy, Wells almost laughed. But when he saw the fury in her eyes, his amusement drained away. "Let them come for me. I'm done playing their games. They act so enlightened, but underneath it, they're rotten to the core." Octavia reached out and took the hand of the girl standing next to her. She had dark curly hair and looked vaguely familiar. "I'm not going to let anyone hurt you," Octavia told her.

"What's going on?" Wells asked, looking from one girl to the other. "What happened?"

"One of the so-called Protectors attacked her. He grabbed her and pulled her down to the ground, saying some bullshit about the Earth wanting them to be together. Thankfully, Anna kicked him in the balls and got away, because she's a warrior." Octavia's expression softened as she looked at the girl, her eyes full of concern.

"Well done, Anna," Wells said slowly. He stared at her. "You look awfully familiar . . ."

Octavia smiled. "She's from Walden."

Wells's heart skidded to a stop. "Walden? You're from the *Colony*?"

She nodded, and for the next few minutes, he listened to Anna's remarkable tale about her journey to Earth, and what happened after her dropship crashed. "What happened to the others?" he asked, slightly dazed. "The ones who weren't taken by the Protectors?"

"I guess they're still out there. They were looking for the rest of you . . . I hope they made it."

Octavia took Anna's hand again. "They will. Or else, we'll go find them, and then we'll all get to have a fresh start together." She smiled. "You're going to love it at our camp. There's a stream where we can go swimming, and this rabbit that comes to visit every morning. And every night, we sit by the fire and talk until it's time to go to sleep."

Anna raised an eyebrow. "And where will I be sleeping?"

"I'm sure we'll find a spot for you somewhere," Octavia said, a gleam in her eye Wells had never seen before.

"I can't wait to see it," Anna said, a note of wistfulness in her voice. She turned to Wells. "Octavia said you might have a plan to help us?"

"I have the start of one," he said, glancing over his shoulder to make sure no one was listening.

"The first step is waiting." Octavia grimaced. "And then followed by some waiting and more waiting."

Before he could glare at her, Wells heard movement behind them. He cleared his throat.

"I was allowed to pledge myself to Earth's service today," he said, more loudly than before.

"That's wonderful," Anna said, catching on instantly and shooting Octavia a look for good measure. "I hope that we'll be allowed to as well."

A woman in gray passed them, glaring at Wells suspiciously.

"If Earth wills it," Octavia said, her head dipped penitently.

They all repeated it, including the gray woman, who moved on.

"You're on your way up, then," Anna said. "You and Glass."

"Glass?" Wells tensed. "What do you mean?"

"She's working as a maid for the High Protector now," Octavia said, her eyebrows rising. "Out of the dorms and into the inner chamber, living in Soren's wing."

Wells's heart started racing. "Which way are Soren's rooms?"

"I'll show you," Octavia said, putting down her laundry.

Octavia led him past the laundry lines, pointing out through an alley to the left. "Follow the gray ladies that way and you'll get there. But I wouldn't hang around if you don't see Glass right away. There are a lot of eyes watching that area."

"Thanks," Wells said, then cocked his head to the side and surveyed Octavia with a playful, appraising look. "So . . . is something going on between you and that Walden girl?"

She pressed her lips together, but couldn't keep a smile from spreading across her face.

"Oh boy . . ." Wells laughed. "There are going to be a lot of heartbroken guys back at the camp." He paused thoughtfully. "Girls too."

"Okay, relax there, Jaha."

"Noted." He sighed. "I'd better get going. Just be careful, okay, O? Make sure you and Anna take care of each other until we find a way out of here."

Octavia glanced over at Anna, who had started hanging the laundry. "We will," she said, her voice a combination of determination and tenderness.

This is good, Wells thought as he hurried away. *I'm rising in the ranks and Glass has access to the inner circle. All the pieces are coming together. Now I just need to—*

There she was . . . Glass, walking with Soren along the outer road, wearing a new white dress, her blond hair clean and loose around her shoulders, her head tilted upward to listen as Soren spoke. She was smiling. She looked, inexplicably, at peace.

Wells felt the ground dropping around him, the walls rising higher, the stomp of feet surrounding him growing louder.

She's just pretending, he told himself. *She's following the plan.*

Glass glanced up, spotting him. Wells blinked at her twice, in signal, then turned and walked away, wondering why his hopeful excitement had suddenly turned to dread.

CHAPTER *17*

Clarke

When Clarke woke up in the early morning, Bellamy was pacing restlessly. He looked so frantic and exhausted it was almost too painful for her to look at him. All she wanted was to wrap her arms around him, to tell him that everything was going to be okay, but this was not the Bellamy she could comfort. She'd learned long ago what to do when he had that feral gleam in his eye, when his muscles twitched with coiled energy.

He and Felix had found something on their scouting mission, and had waited for everyone to wake up to fill them in. Bellamy waited for Vale to stagger over, sleepily rubbing her eyes, then launched in without preamble.

"We've found a back door into these people's entire stash of weapons," he said. His eyes shone with a manic intensity that made Clarke shiver.

Felix stood a few feet behind him, arms crossed tight. "And they have no idea it's there," he added. "We might not have long before they discover the hole."

No, Clarke thought desperately. *That's not the way to do this.* They were vastly outnumbered. Weapons weren't going to help them here. They had to try diplomacy, offer some kind of trade. There had to be something these people wanted, or else they wouldn't have attacked their camp.

Clarke glanced at Paul, who had an unusually grave look on his face. He and Clarke had discussed this last night with the others, while Felix and Bellamy had gone off on their own. He'd back her up.

"The walls look unbreakable, but only from a distance," Bellamy went on. Clarke noticed that his hands were shaking. "There are windows, cracked foundations, places we could plant these explosives and blow the whole thing down around them."

"You know this *how*, exactly?" Paul asked, smiling tightly. "Did you become an engineer in the past two days, on top of everything else?"

Instinctively, Clarke started to rise to Bellamy's defense, but Bellamy's eyes lit up, smirk back in place.

"No, I'm not an engineer," he said calmly. "But he is."

He nodded to Luke, who was sitting on a log, his forehead creasing as he listened.

"What do you think, Luke?" Bellamy asked. "Is this viable?"

"I'd have to see it for myself," he said, scratching his curly hair. "Help figure out where to position the explosives."

Bellamy nodded. "That was going to be my next suggestion. We can risk one more recon trip, maybe tonight . . ."

Clarke stood.

"Then we'll loot the armory and—"

"And blow up part of the building," Clarke finished for him. "With our *friends* inside."

Bellamy fell silent, turning to look at her.

She tried to ignore the look on his face, a mixture of pain and frustration. "This is reckless and this is wrong."

"*Thank* you," Paul said, standing up beside her with a huff. "I was sitting here listening to this, wondering if I was the only one who—"

Clarke cut him off, her eyes never leaving Bellamy's. "We have to try diplomacy first, Bel. We have no idea where our friends are inside this . . . this structure, fortress, whatever you want to call it. For all we know, they could be in *exactly* the places you're planning to bomb."

Bellamy stiffened. "I thought about that," he said

through clenched teeth. "Those walls are just a defense. If we can knock them down, we can get to the heart of the structure without putting our friends at risk."

Clarke took a deep breath. She knew Bellamy wouldn't like it, but she had to speak. "Why do we have to attack at all?" she asked, turning to face the others. "Shouldn't we explore *every* option available to us?"

Bellamy let out a short, bitter laugh. "You really think talking to these monsters is an option?"

Clarke blinked hard, trying to avoid the scorn in his face. "Paul and I talked about this last night. We think there's a way to make a tactical and peaceful approach that will allow our loved ones to come home safely. We will listen to the demands of these . . . raiders."

"These murderers," Bellamy shot back.

"And we will offer a counterproposal, keeping the lines of communication open as long as we can in the hopes of a peaceful solution. Meanwhile, we can use that time to come up with a plan B that might be a little less . . ." She turned away from Bellamy, bracing herself for his reaction. "Rash. More strategically viable."

Even without looking, she could feel the anger radiating from him. "And if our friends are killed in the meantime?" Bellamy asked, striding toward her. "My brother. My little *sister*? Are you really prepared to gamble with their lives?"

"Are *you*?" Clarke's voice rose, her fists balling with anger. She refused to let him make her feel like some callous, uncaring person just because she wanted to exercise caution. "Because that's what you're bringing to us right now, Bel! A huge, reckless, crazy gamble."

"*Crazy*," Bellamy repeated. "You really want to throw that word at me right now?"

"You know what's crazy?" Paul said. "Risking our lives to save people who might already be dead."

The word sucked the air out of the woods around them. Cooper winced, and next to her, Clarke saw Jessa go pale.

Paul threw his hands up. "I'm just saying what everybody's thinking! That's a variable we need to keep in mind. There's no sense in putting our own lives at risk until we know that there are people left in there to save."

"They're not dead," Bellamy said in a low, dangerous voice. "And I'm not going to stand here while you cowards come up with excuses to abandon them."

Vale cleared her throat. "He has a point. We're working with limited information. We need to gather more before we can make a—"

"*You* might need to. But I don't." Bellamy turned around and started away, waving for Felix to follow. "We know where the armory is. We can take it from here."

"No!" Clarke shouted, hurrying after him. "Bellamy,

you can't. This will put everything at risk . . . their *lives* at risk, you've got to see that!"

When he turned, his eyes were cold. "The only thing I see is a bunch of cowards, too scared to do what they swore to do." He scanned the others quickly; then his gaze darted back to Clarke, pinning her with a glare. "Or is *selfish* a better word?"

She tried to reply, but couldn't. Her chest was too tight, her heart aching, her blood too hot.

Bellamy turned away again, nodding at Luke. "You coming?"

Luke half rose, then looked to Clarke, wavering. She mouthed, *please*, and he sat back down.

Bellamy snorted. "That's fine. I'll wing it."

"No, you won't," Paul said. "Stand down, Bellamy."

"I'm not one of your guards," Bellamy snapped. "And I think you mean *Councilor Blake*."

Frustration bubbled up hot in Clarke's chest. "Is that what this is really all about, Bellamy?" she asked. "You don't feel like you're getting the respect you deserve? Are you really going to endanger our friends' lives to prove a point?"

His face turned white. "I'm trying to *save* them," he spat. "We have no idea what's going on in there—" He pointed toward the fortress. "They could be torturing

Wells. Octavia could be in pain. And you're all just content to sit there, doing nothing."

"You're not the only one who's worried about someone you love," Jessa snapped, stepping forward. "We're all desperate for this mission to be a success. But we only have one shot, and we have to make it count."

"I *will* make it count," Bellamy said through gritted teeth. "But if we wait any longer, it could be too late. So here's how it's going to work. Anyone who's ready to rescue our friends, come with me."

"No," Paul said. "I'm sorry, Bellamy, I get where you're coming from, but it's the wrong move. You're not going anywhere."

"And how the hell do you plan to stop me?"

Paul pulled something metallic out of his pocket: a pair of the restraints that Clarke was painfully familiar with, the same ones they'd used back on the ship. The same ones Rhodes had used to bring them before a firing squad.

"What are you doing with those?" Clarke asked, her heart beating fast.

Paul glanced over at her. "I came prepared."

"Give them to me," Clarke said, extending her arm. "You're being ridiculous."

Paul shook his head gravely. "I know all about your boyfriend, Clarke. Wherever he goes, chaos ensues. I was there when he got the Chancellor shot. He's a live wire, and I'm not going to let him get anyone killed again."

"You're not tying him up either," Clarke said, stepping forward to stand in between Paul and Bellamy.

"That won't be an issue," Bellamy said, eyes flashing. "I'm out of here. Let's go, Felix."

"This is the wrong move," Paul said, his voice growing louder as he looked imploringly at Jessa, Cooper, and Vale. "You saw what happened the last time you listened to Bellamy. Your people took him in and *died* for it. Do you really want to let him run off and use those weapons without exhausting our other options first?"

"Paul's right," Cooper said gruffly. "We should wait."

But Bellamy ignored him and started walking away.

Paul nodded at Cooper, and in a flash, they'd grabbed Bellamy's arms and wrenched them behind his back.

"Get off of me!" Bellamy spat, thrashing from side to side.

"Let him go!" Clarke cried out, dashing over to them. "You're hurting him." She grabbed on to Paul's arm, but he shoved her off easily.

"This is insane," Luke said, hurrying over and reaching out to help Bellamy, but Vale grabbed Luke and pulled him back. Still weakened from his injury and the long hike, he didn't have the strength to fight her off.

"Let him go *right now*," Clarke said in a voice that made Felix jump.

The restraints in place, Cooper was able to hold Bellamy on his own, allowing Paul to turn to Clarke. "It's okay, Clarke. We're just going to wait until he calms down and sees reason. Then we'll let him go."

Clarke turned to Bellamy, to make it clear that she wasn't going to stand for this mutiny. But when their eyes locked, she didn't recognize the person facing her. He was looking at her with such fury that a wave of fear rippled through her. No. They couldn't let him loose in this condition. He'd get himself killed, and bring everyone else down with him. Wells and Octavia included. They had to get him to see reason, even if it meant doing something unforgivable.

"I'm sorry." The words burned as they left her throat, and she turned away, her heart cracking under the weight of her shame.

Bellamy fell into a stony silence as they led him past Clarke. She froze, waiting for his eyes to reach hers, sharp with accusation—but they didn't even graze her.

As if he couldn't even bear to look at her.

CHAPTER *18*

Bellamy

The hours crept by painfully, and Bellamy sat in silence. Eventually, the sun went down. With no fire and no lantern, Bellamy's eyes had had time to adjust to the dark. He saw the night birds swooping on their way to search for prey. He saw bugs scuttling past in the soil. And in the near distance, he saw the path the raiders had cut through the forest with their wagons, dragging his family and friends with them.

He'd never felt so alone in his entire life.

He'd been secured to one of the metal beams and his back ached against it. His breathing had gotten slower at least, since that first wave of pure panic had passed. He'd stopped shaking and sweating and his heart no longer felt as if it was about to explode inside his chest.

But he wasn't okay. He was never going to be okay again.

Bellamy shifted his weight, feeling the cuffs cutting into his wrists once again. They hurt, but nothing stung like the memory of Clarke standing by as her new buddy Paul dragged Bellamy away.

A twig cracked and Bellamy's back stiffened. He sensed her before he saw her.

"Bellamy," Clarke said softly. "Are you okay? I brought you some food." She took a few hesitant steps, as though she were approaching a wounded animal, and crouched, leaning forward to place her hand on his arm.

Bellamy recoiled, wrenching himself as far from her as possible. "Don't you dare touch me."

"I just wanted to take off the restraints so you could eat," she said, her voice shaking. She drew her hand back and watched him for a moment, settling into the dirt a few feet away. "I'm sorry things got . . . out of hand today."

"Out of hand?" he repeated, feeling rage boil up inside again. "You stood there while Paul staged a coup. But it's okay, I get it. He's more useful to you now than I am."

Her brow furrowed. "What are you talking about?"

"Let's see," he said, pretending to be deep in thought. "First you dated the Chancellor's son, which I don't blame you for. Always a good idea to aim high when you can. But then Wells wasn't very popular on Earth at first, was he?" He made an exaggerated grimace. "I wasn't very popular either, but I could hunt, so I guess it was a smart trade. You knew you wouldn't starve. Temporary, though. You hardly expected to spend the rest of your life with a piece of Walden trash like me. And then, here comes *Paul*, with his officer training and his smooth-talking, ass-kissing charm, and you realized that it was time to upgrade again."

Clarke's mouth fell open as she stared at him with a combination of shock and disgust. After a long moment, her eyes narrowed and she spoke. "You see, *this* is why we don't want you part of the negotiations tomorrow. You let your temper take over, and then you start to believe your own crazy stories. It's dangerous."

Bellamy scoffed. "Yeah? So tell me. What's your big plan for tomorrow?"

She raised her chin. "I'm going to approach the entrance holding a white flag. We're not sure whether they have that custom, but it's worth a try. And I'll ask to speak to their leader to negotiate the terms of release."

Her words knocked the anger from his chest. "What? No, Clarke, you *can't*. They'll shoot you before you even have a chance to open your mouth."

Clarke crossed her arms over her chest. "It's our only

option. We don't have the weapons to make a strategic attack—"

"We can use *their* weapons. I told you!" A note of desperation crept into his voice. The hurt and fury he'd felt was gone, replaced by cold dread. He couldn't let her do this.

"And I told *you*. We can't blow up part of the building. Not when we have no idea where the prisoners are being kept."

"Clarke, please . . ." His voice cracked. "Don't do it. After everything . . . if I lose you too . . ."

She raised her chin, eyes blazing. "When are you finally going to understand? Just because you love someone, it doesn't give you the moral right to do something unreasonable. We're all scared. We're all in pain. But we have to be rational."

Her exaggerated calmness reignited the smoldering anger. She was treating him like one of her patients in the psychiatric unit on the ship. Like he was too delusional to understand what was really going on. No matter what, she'd always see him as some hotheaded fool who stormed into situations and made everything worse. He wasn't going to let her make him feel that way.

He felt his lips curl into a sneer. "People die while you're trying to be *rational*, Clarke. Like Lily." He knew the words were a step over the line the moment they came out of his mouth.

She recoiled and gasped, as if his words had knocked the air out of her. "Are you serious?" she said hoarsely. Years ago, her parents had been blackmailed into performing experiments with radiation on children, as part of the Council's attempt to determine whether Earth could support human life. Bellamy's first girlfriend, Lily, had been one of the subjects, and although Clarke had done everything she could to save her, it hadn't been enough.

"I'm just saying that you might not be the best person to determine our course of action when there are lives on the line."

Her head shot up, rage, hurt, pain shining from her eyes. Then, as Bellamy watched, his chest growing tight, she pulled it all back in, her face becoming as cold and remote as a statue.

"And you are?" she snapped. "The last time you were involved in a hostage situation, your father was shot."

He stared at her, finding it hard to believe that this was the same girl who'd left the safety of their camp to go with him to find Octavia when she went missing. The girl who trusted him, who needed him . . . who loved him.

"Just . . . go," he said. "Go do whatever you think is best and I'll do the same."

"Fine." She spun around and left without another word.

The silence that settled over the camp felt absolute. His eyelids fluttered and fell and he swore he could feel Octavia's tiny hand holding his as they hid together in their cabin on the ship, Wells's arms wrapping around him the first time they embraced as brothers, Clarke's body warm against his as they stared up at the stars.

All things that were about to be stolen from him tomorrow, when Clarke put her suicidal plan into action.

CHAPTER 19

Glass

Yesterday had been the kind of busy day that leaves you floating just above dreams all night long, your body longing to stay in motion. In the darkness of her chamber, Glass's mind flitted from memory to memory, never quite settling into deep slumber.

It had started with a rude awakening, being dragged out of the dorms to become Soren's new maid, but it had ended on a very different note, with a dinner of delicious, spiced stew, surrounded by Soren and her advisors, their warm chatter and laughter filling the chamber.

Over the course of the day, there had been visits to nearly every corner of the compound; Soren drawing up plans for planting in several areas surrounding the outer walls; ducking into the sorting area, where the women were dividing goods up to keep or to melt down or scrap; walking along the river's edge, where some of the men were teaching the younger members of the group to catch fish. They'd even paid a visit to the barracks, so that the High Protector could congratulate some of the newer recruits on their training and wish them well.

Glass hadn't seen any of her friends there, and was secretly a little relieved about it. She'd spotted Wells only briefly, passing through the outer corridors of the Stone, and had flushed with panic at the sight of him, without really even knowing why.

She was almost enjoying herself. She felt useful here, in a way she hadn't the entire time they'd been on Earth. Maybe in her whole life. She'd trailed Soren all day long, providing water when she was thirsty, a cloak when she was cold, taking notes on scraps of parchment after Soren learned that Glass could write. But mostly Glass watched and listened . . . and learned. She was amazed at how Soren could be both powerful and beloved—a far cry from the leaders she'd known back on the Colony. And she couldn't stop herself from imagining, someday, having people look at her with the same reverence.

But could she do that if she returned to the camp? What

future was waiting there for her? Yet anytime her thoughts drifted in that direction, a face materialized in her mind. Luke. The warm, sleepy smile that greeted her the moment she woke up in the morning. The way his brown eyes crinkled when she made him laugh. The look of fear and anguish when he shouted at her to run.

But now it was the beginning of a new day, and Glass lay in her bed in the anteroom attached to Soren's chamber, physically exhausted but half-awake, waiting for her next set of orders. After all, Margot had said that Soren kept odd hours. She might call for Glass at any moment. She needed to be—

She stirred, hearing a voice in the chamber beyond. Was this a summons? Through her little window, she could see a corner of sky and it was still dark, but now she heard a few low voices rising up from Soren's room. Glass rose quietly and slipped from her nightgown into her white dress. If Soren and her advisors were awake, they'd call for her soon.

Glass had almost finished braiding her hair when she heard one of the advisors say her name. She hurried to the door that separated her room from Soren's but some gut instinct made her hesitate before opening it. She stopped instead and listened.

"If she hadn't spoken up that day . . ." It sounded like Margot's voice.

"Yes, Glass would have stayed among the other female recruits." This was Soren. The other voices fell silent as she spoke. "That's why she was chosen in the first place, but I feel she'll be more *useful* in our ranks. She has an aptitude. I also have the feeling that she may not pair well."

"No?" Margot asked.

Glass held her breath, bracing herself into the corner of the room so she wouldn't move, her ear turned toward the tiny crack in the doorframe. "Pair well"? What did *that* mean?

"I sense an attachment elsewhere," Soren said briskly. "She's in love and she's holding on to it still. It closes her off to men, but it opens her up to Earth. To us. So we'll have to be very considerate about her pairing."

Glass's hands flew to her chest. How could Soren know that?

"Anyhow, aside from our new friend, we'll keep the ranks as they stand," Soren said. There was a shuffle, like the others were rising from their seats. "We'll finalize the pairings tomorrow so the first rites will be as fruitful as possible, if Earth wills it."

"If Earth wills it," they all repeated back. It sounded like there were four or five of them in there with her.

They hadn't called for Glass yet. She probably wasn't meant to have heard this, whatever this was. But even as her mind swam, her instincts kicked in. She scrambled out of her dress and back into her nightgown as quickly and quietly as she could, back under the covers, her eyes closing just as she heard the door swing open and Dara's soft voice call out, "Glass? You're needed."

Glass rose slowly, feigning grogginess. "I'm sorry. How long have I . . . ?"

Dara smiled sympathetically from the doorway. "You'll get used to this. Take a few minutes. We'll be out here when you're ready."

This time, Glass didn't rush to get dressed. She was still straightening her hem as she emerged from the room, hoping she looked flushed from sleep instead of from panic.

"I'm sorry I didn't wake up sooner," she said, taking in the room. There were six of the gray women here, it turned out, all clustered around Soren, who sat by the crackling hearth on a thick woolen rug. "I'm ready now."

Soren peered over her shoulder with a kind smile, and patted the empty spot on the rug beside her. "Come and sit."

Glass obeyed, lowering herself into the tiny space next to Soren.

"Did you get some rest?" the High Protector asked pleasantly.

Glass forced a smile. "Yes, thank you."

"I'm glad to hear it. There are some very exciting things

in the works, events that I sincerely hope you'll be a part of. We're preparing for our next Pairing Ceremony—one of our most sacred rituals."

For once, Glass didn't have to feign an interested gleam in her eye. "What is it?"

"Well, first I need to tell you a little bit about our people's history. May I tell you a story?"

Glass nodded, and Soren continued. "The early Protectors had taken refuge in shelters far to the west, where the mountains are tall and the wilderness much more brutal than even here." Soren's voice took on a melodic quality, as though she was reciting a story she'd told hundreds of times before. Glass felt drowsy and cozy hearing it, as if she were being tucked into a blanket with every word.

"They lived under the ground for a time, while Earth healed Herself, but there weren't enough supplies to sustain them for long. They emerged too early." Her tone darkened, her mouth pinched with sympathy. "The air was toxic, the water impure. They only remained on the surface for a few days before they realized how dire the situation was. They needed to return to the sheltering arms of Earth. But where and how? Just as they began to despair, Earth sent them a vision . . . a ray of light leading east. It was only a matter of hours before they found it."

"Found what?" Glass asked eagerly.

"Earth's gift," Soren said, smiling. "The door to another shelter, its lock corroded by the very air that was making them ill. They opened it easily and found food, water, enough provisions for another fifty years."

Glass debated asking, but found she couldn't resist. "Were there people inside already?"

Soren nodded gravely. "There were. Some were amazed by the story the Protectors told of how they found their salvation. Those new friends were brought into the fold as faithful servants. Others were angry that the Protectors had stepped into their shelter. They wanted to drive them out, back to certain death. Those people . . . had to be subdued."

Though this had happened generations ago, there was a little note of regret in Soren's voice, as if she were the one who'd made that decision. She must have been feeling the weight of her role in telling this story—the heavy mantle the High Protectors had worn for so long.

"Once they joined with their new followers, the shelter found peace and equilibrium," Soren went on, more cheerfully. "No divisions. No strife. And it's been that way ever since . . . for the faithful. In the old world, society was broken down into component parts, arbitrary things, really. Us versus them. My color against your color. My family unit feuding with yours." She waved her hand in the air, eyes glittering. "We've done away with all that. There are no families but *our one* family. As Protectors, we are mothers to all our people's children. Now, every time the Earth shows us a new home, we perform the Pairing Ceremony and officially welcome our newest members into our family as Protectors."

"I . . . I suppose I understand that," Glass said, though she had a sinking feeling that Soren was still keeping something from her. Though she'd told Glass about the Protectors' history, she somehow skirted around the issue about what exactly the Pairing Ceremony was.

Soren turned to the other women, who were raising their eyebrows as if impressed. "This is what I meant by aptitude, you see?" She pivoted again, squeezing Glass's hands with her own. "Glass, I think you're going to play a very important role in this community. I'm so glad we get the chance to officially welcome you at the Pairing Ceremony. You'll like that, right?"

Glass nodded politely, though her mind had started whirring. Whatever Soren was keeping from her still, Glass had a bad, bad feeling about it. She had to warn Octavia, Anna, and the others. They had to find Wells and tell them the time had come. She'd find a way out, no matter what it took.

CHAPTER 20

Wells

Wells lined up with his fellow captives in the early-morning light. While the Protectors walked up and down the line, he stood at attention, chin raised proudly, his mouth set in a tepid smile, just like the others.

Eric, Graham, and Kit were still playing along, of course. As were the other seven recruits from their camp. But for all Wells knew, the other dozen male recruits were true converts. They were Earthborns, though not from Max's village, or part of the group that'd split off. It made his mind spin, thinking about how many other hidden communities there could be . . . people who'd found different ways to survive the Cataclysm. Once this was all over, he was going to learn about them all.

Oak stepped forward to address the gathering. There seemed to be only a loose hierarchy among the Protectors, but Wells had gotten the sense of a pecking order among them, with Oak near the very top.

"Today, we're doing something different," Oak boomed. "Some of you will be leaving the Stone to go do Earth's will."

Oak turned away, taking something from one of the other Protectors. In one quick blink, he was in front of Wells, holding out a rifle. There was a strange intensity in his eyes. Wells knew even before he took the gun from Oak that it was loaded.

At the first touch of cool metal, his heart started pounding so loud he swore everyone around him could hear it. He nodded sharply and stood with his gun across his chest, the way they'd trained him to, as Oak continued down the line, arming the other recruits for whatever today's mission would be.

Oak stopped three men down, at Graham, pausing with a squint before handing the gun over. Graham gave a nod and Oak stomped away, pointing to the others, who hadn't been given weapons, including Eric and Kit.

"The rest of you will remain with me for further

target training. Wish your brothers luck today on their mission."

As the others murmured, "Luck be with you, if Earth wills it," Wells realized what was happening in slow, gradual bursts.

He was going out on a mission.

He was going *out* . . . leaving this compound.

He was holding a loaded rifle.

Wells turned and saw Graham realizing the same thing. A trickle of sweat rolled down Graham's forehead, despite the chilly air.

Graham's finger twitched against the rifle's trigger, his eyes traveling to Wells's and holding there, pleading. Wells shook his head—this morning wasn't the moment, their friends weren't even heading out with them—but before he could mouth, *not today*, another Protector with eerie blue eyes stepped up and began to give orders.

"I'll be leading today's expedition," the Protector called, crossing his arms over his chest. "This will be very simple. In and out. We don't anticipate any altercations today. We'll be heading out to a farm site we've discovered near here to bolster our food stores for the winter. One hour by wagon, one hour there, one hour back. Any questions?"

A farm site. Wells still couldn't get over the fact that there were other people here on Earth, not too far from his own camp. People with *farms*. He knew he should keep his mouth shut, but the offer was out there, and he did have a question. A big one. He raised his hand.

The blue-eyed Protector nodded at him. "Yes?"

"How can you be sure there won't be any altercations?" he asked.

"We can't be sure of anything." The Protector blinked. "But the farm is, as of now, unoccupied. There shouldn't be anyone there to oppose us."

How can they know that? Wells wondered, but he nodded once and kept that question to himself, as they shouldered their weapons and stepped into a new set of horse-drawn wagons. This time they sat on the Protectors' benches instead of being tied up on the floor. *They must have scouted this farm*, Wells realized as he sat down, *just like they spied on my camp before taking us.*

But if that were the case, why wouldn't the Protectors have just gone in and looted then? Something wasn't adding up about this mission.

The wagons rolled down a dirt road carved out of the rubble-strewn landscape, and Wells looked out the high windows to try to get his bearings. The morning sun was behind him, so they must have been heading north.

Good, Wells thought, glancing anxiously at Graham. If they'd headed back west, instead of into brand-new territory, Graham might have been tempted to make a break for it. *I might have been tempted myself.*

But that would mean leaving Eric and Kit behind, along with Glass, Octavia, and the others. It would mean risking large-scale retaliation. It wouldn't solve anything.

After what felt like far less than an hour, the wagon rolled into a low valley and creaked to a stop.

Wells could smell it the second he stepped out into the crisp autumn air: charred wood . . . and something worse. As he turned to face the clearing beyond the wagon, his throat clenched tight.

So this was why they'd called it a *farm site*, instead of a farm. It wasn't just their odd Protector terminology, it was the truth. This was a place where a farm *used* to be. Now it was just a burned-out field. In the center, there was the smoldering wreckage of what was once a homestead.

Wells stared at the far side of the site, disgust pooling in his stomach. The dirt was overturned there, loose and choppy, forming a wide, messy hill. Wells didn't need to ask what that mound covered. The answer was in the blood still staining the grass around him. It was a mass grave.

They knew no one was here because they'd made sure of it.

"We had to wait for the fire to go out to search further," the Protector said from behind Wells, the man's eerily soft voice making him jump. He pointed over Wells's shoulder at the desiccated heap where the building once stood. "There's a cellar in the center that should be well stocked. Take whatever the fire didn't destroy and load it in the carts."

Wells couldn't quite get the words "yes, sir" out, but this Protector didn't seem to require it. He had already turned away, directing the others toward the remnants of the farm.

Wells started to shake more and more visibly the closer he got to the building. He wondered whether this was the real test. Were the Protectors bringing them here as a reminder of what they'd done to the recruits' homes? Was this what Wells's own camp looked like now, completely obliterated, the people who had lived there now buried in a heap of dirt?

Graham strode up beside him, his jaw clenched. He glanced at Wells darkly. Wells couldn't muster a nod, a head shake, anything.

They marched together, fists clenched tight around their guns, to the center of the farmhouse, stepping gingerly over crumbling foundations and blackened beams. The two Protectors overseeing them watched unblinkingly from the wagon.

One of the other recruits walked nervously into the building, then gave a shout as his leg fell through the weakened floor. Wells hurried silently over to pull him out, looking into the boy's eyes as he hoisted him up and patted him on the shoulder. This recruit had been there when Wells had arrived, but Wells had no idea what his name was, where he came from, or how he felt about all this, except that he looked white-knuckle terrified right now.

"Thanks, man," the boy whispered, gripping his gun with sweaty hands as Wells nodded and moved away.

"It's here," Graham called, pointing downward with his rifle.

Wells made his way over. There was a rusted metal grate in the floor, and when they heaved it open, it revealed a poured-cement stairwell, still intact.

"Let's just get this over with," Wells said under his breath and started down, leading the way.

In the dusty light spilling down from above, Wells could make out shelves stocked with unmarked tins. Nets hung from the ceiling, full of potatoes, turnips, and other root vegetables, and a briny smell from the far corner probably meant there were cured meats and fish stocked here for the winter as well.

As Wells stepped closer to the shelves, ready to load up and get out of here as quickly as possible, his foot touched something soft. He leaned down to see what it was, but

Graham was already beside him, stooping, pulling it up.

They both stood and stared at it in thick silence. It was a teddy bear, worn through in patches, its stitched mouth set in a deep frown.

A child had lived here.

Graham looked at Wells, eyes burning with rage. He dropped the teddy bear onto the ground. Then he turned and barreled back up the stairs, pulling his rifle off his shoulder and into position.

Wells felt the click of Graham's safety like a snap in his own brain. He drew a scalding breath and raced after him.

"Graham, don't!" he screamed, but it was too late.

Graham was sprinting out of the building, letting out a guttural wordless scream that echoed throughout the valley. A shot rang out, Graham's course wavering a little from the kickback. Wells stared up at the two Protectors, ducking with their hands over their shaved heads, and reached for his own rifle, frantically wondering which direction to point it in. If Graham had hit one of them, he could get the other . . .

Graham fired again. It ricocheted off the side of the wagon, and Wells could see the spot his first bullet had hit. He'd missed both times. The Protectors were up and running, one of them zigzagging, luring Graham closer while the other looped around behind Graham, tackling him to the ground, disarming him effortlessly while shoving something into his back.

A sedative, Wells realized, his rifle dipping useless in his hands. *Just like when they got us in the first place.*

"Get him in the wagon," the blue-eyed Protector called out to the other one, his voice as hollowed of emotion as ever. Then he turned his gun on Wells. "Drop your guns, all of you."

Wells let go of his rifle, watched it plummet into the dirt and staggered backward, hands up high. Out of the corner of his eye, he could see the other two prisoners follow suit.

"Good," said the Protector, his eyes drifting past them. "Now finish up and let's get going."

Wells glanced behind him, surprised, then blinked hard and hurried back to the cellar as ordered. They acted so nonchalant, like this happened all the time. Maybe it did. Maybe they'd known one of them would crack.

Wells gritted his teeth so hard his jaw ached as he loaded the vehicle with food. When it was done, he and the others ducked back into the wagon, where the Protectors had left them room on the bench.

Graham was sprawled unconscious on the floor

beneath them. One of the Protectors casually used his lifeless shoulder as a footrest the entire way back to the Stone.

When they stopped in the courtyard, the blue-eyed Protector put his hand up, stopping Wells. "Drag your friend to the kennels."

"He's not my friend," Wells said. "And I'd be happy to."

The words tasted like poison in his mouth, but the Protector smiled, appeased. Wells drew a breath and reached into the wagon to hoist Graham into his arms.

"Did I tell you to carry him?" the Protector asked coolly. "Huh. I could have sworn I said to *drag* him." He walked slowly behind Wells, raised his gun, and dug its barrel between Wells's shoulder blades.

Wells felt wrath pulse through his veins, a volcano due to explode at any moment, but his fear was even stronger. One squeeze of that trigger and he wouldn't be able to help Graham or Octavia or Glass or anyone ever again.

"Yes, sir," he said. Carefully, he laid Graham onto the ground and started to pull, while the Protector's gun dug into his back, prodding him step by step, straight into the belly of the Stone.

Soon, he thought. There was no more waiting for the perfect time, for the ideal intel, to bring these people to their knees. They were going to have to get out of there. *The next chance we get.*

If there *was* a next chance.

Wells dared one last longing glance back at the open sky, tugging Graham behind him, before the mammoth walls swallowed them both up again.

CHAPTER *21*

Clarke

There wasn't much she could do to prepare. She wasn't bringing any weapons, of course. And she wasn't bringing anything to trade. Unless there was some kind of gift she could offer as a sign of goodwill? Images of white-clad men flashed through her mind—their blank, expressionless faces as they methodically scoured the camp, ignoring the cries and screams of those who'd been injured in the explosion.

No, these weren't the type of people who could be swayed with gifts. They would respond to strength. And bravery.

As Clarke paced back and forth, nervously running her

hands along the rough bark of the trees, she tried to picture herself approaching the giant concrete wall, her head held high. She had to look like an equal, not a victim. She'd imagine Wells was watching her from inside, and that she had to make him proud.

And maybe, just maybe, they'd listen to her and release the prisoners. She could already see the look on Bellamy's face when he saw Clarke with Octavia. His stony expression would collapse, replaced by joy and relief. And after hugging his sister, he'd turn to Clarke with gratitude in his eyes.

A branch snapped, and Clarke whirled around to see Paul coming toward her. "I'm ready," she said, squaring her shoulders. "I think I should head out now."

"There's been a change of plans," he said cheerfully, as if they were discussing a trip to swim in the creek instead of a potentially fatal rescue mission. "Cooper is going to go instead, and Vale is going to go watch to make sure it goes okay. She'll return when he's safely inside. It makes more sense for an Earthborn to act as the negotiator. Cooper will have more in common with them, and then we don't have to worry about all the hostility toward the people who dropped out of the sky."

"What? A change of plans? When did you discuss this?" Clarke craned her head, looking for signs that a meeting had just broken up.

"It was my decision," Paul said. He placed his hand on Clarke's shoulder and looked her straight in the eye. "I don't want you to think I don't have faith in you, because I do. I hope you know how much we all appreciate you."

Her confusion sizzling into anger, Clarke shoved his hand off and stepped to the side. "*Your* decision? Paul, no one put you in charge."

He chuckled and shook his head. "Leadership isn't something that's assigned, Clarke. It's earned. Given as a gift by those who willingly follow you. I think it's pretty clear who everyone trusts here. Cooper, Vale, Felix, Jessa—they're all counting on me to make this operation a success, so I've made some changes. Besides, we need you back here in case anyone gets hurt."

Clarke stared at him for a moment, trying to glean information from his beaming smile. "Okay . . ." she said slowly, trying to stay calm as she assessed the situation. "I'll wait here, then. I'm going to go wish Cooper and Vale good luck before they head off."

"They've already left! Now all we can do is hope for the best."

———

The next couple of hours were tense, and they all took turns guarding their makeshift campsite. While Felix was on duty, Clarke came up to bring him some berries she'd found in the woods.

"Thanks," Felix said with a weak smile, "but there's no way I can eat right now."

"It's weird, isn't it?" Clarke said. "Knowing how close we are to them right now? I wonder if they can sense us coming."

"I hope so." Felix turned away, biting his lip. "I can't stand the thought of him scared, or in pain, or . . ." He trailed off.

"I've never seen Eric scared," Clarke said firmly. "I'll bet he's being strong and brave, just like he always is."

When Felix turned back, there were tears glistening in his eyes. "I'm sure he is." He wiped his eyes with the back of his hand. "I just hope he knows we haven't given up on them."

"I'm sure he knows that," Clarke said, glancing over her shoulder toward their camp, where Bellamy was still shackled to the pile of rusty metal. "That's not what we do."

Clarke gave the edge of the camp a wide berth as she walked around it. She would just take a quick peek at Bellamy . . . long enough to know he was bearing up okay, short enough to avoid the feeling of her heart ripping out of her chest, that stabbing sensation that crept up on her pretty much every time she thought about him.

She'd expected to see him sleeping or staring dead-eyed into the treetops while Jessa guarded him from a distance, like an hour ago, the last time she'd peeked. But this time, Jessa was crouched beside Bellamy, near enough to touch him, their heads leaning close as they spoke in hushed murmurs.

Clarke started, stumbling a little where she stood. It was stupid. It was nothing. And yet, it was such a strangely intimate scene that Clarke felt her stomach churn with a mixture of hurt and betrayal. Not that she had any right to feel betrayed after what she'd done to him.

Jessa glanced over her shoulder and Clarke rearranged her face into something approaching neutral. But if it was for Bellamy's benefit, she shouldn't have bothered. He turned away without so much as a blink in her direction as Jessa rose, crossing over to Clarke in four long strides.

"Is Vale back yet?" the Earthborn girl asked brusquely.

Clarke had to swallow to find her voice again, recovering from the feeling of having had it punched out of her throat. "Not yet. Soon, we hope."

"And if she doesn't come back? If neither of them do, what then?" Jessa's voice rose, and Bellamy's head tilted casually toward them, clearly listening. So this must've been what they were talking about. "Do we go with Bellamy's plan?"

"I . . . I'm not sure . . ." Clarke's skin grew prickly hot as she shifted uneasily.

"Because I for one am getting pretty tired of sitting around here doing nothing." Jessa pointed east. "My brother is in that building, maybe alive, maybe dead, I don't know. All I know is, the longer we wait, the worse his odds are."

"I realize that," Clarke said quietly.

"Do you?" Jessa's dark eyes locked with hers. "Then what's our plan B? What do we do now, *tonight*, if negotiations fall apart?"

Bellamy turned and fixed Clarke with a stare—his expression totally empty, as though she was just one of the trees in the forest.

"She's back!" Paul's voice rang out way too loud, echoing through the forest, sending birds scattering from their perches, but for once, Clarke didn't care.

Because Paul sounded happy.

Her pulse raced with hope as she ran toward the campsite, Jessa on her heels. But before they'd taken two steps, Vale and Paul intercepted them, Paul tugging the panting Earthborn behind him by the elbow.

"Tell her!" he said, exultant.

"Cooper . . . he did it like we . . . planned," Vale got out between huffs, managing a faint smile. "He walked up. They came out . . . with guns . . ."

Clarke waited for her to catch her breath, trying to be patient.

"But they saw that he was unarmed . . . so they lowered them," Vale said.

Clarke exhaled.

Vale glanced at Paul. "I wasn't close enough to hear what they said, but they listened to him and they opened the door and walked with him into the building. No cuffs, no violence. So far, so good. Now I guess we wait to see what they say."

Clarke felt her whole body tingle in a waterfall of relief. She drew a breath to thank Vale, but before she could get the words out, Paul lunged for her and wrapped Clarke up in a hug so tight, it lifted her heels off the ground.

"It's working," he said into her ear, then planted a kiss on her cheek. "We're gonna get them back."

As Paul turned away to clap a hand on Vale's back and lead her toward the heart of the campsite, Clarke wiped her cheek dry, fighting a shudder that was partly nerves, partly something new.

He's just an enthusiastic guy, she told herself. *He got caught up in the moment.*

She felt eyes on her back and turned to see Bellamy watching her with an inscrutable expression.

There came that stabbing feeling again, a sharp pain

that started between her ribs and bloomed into something that would destroy her if she let it.

She wouldn't let it.

She blinked back at Bellamy, chin high, and walked away.

CHAPTER 22

Bellamy

Bellamy's body felt as if it was full of glass shards. His arms were aching, his wrists raw meat, his spine wrenched crookedly against the metal beam that held him. But none of that compared to the pain he felt watching Clarke turn her back on him again.

Bellamy had been watching Paul this whole time. He wasn't the cheerful team player he pretended to be. He was a manipulative snake who had his eyes on Clarke.

I need to warn her, he thought, before remembering that Clarke was no longer his responsibility. She'd made that much clear.

He longed to watch her as she walked away, but Bellamy

forced his eyes into the forest instead, holding them open so everything became painfully sharp and bright, his emotions taking a backseat to the stark realities before him.

In the forest, something moved—a person. Bellamy tensed; then he released a breath. Luke stepped out from behind a tree, lifting his hand in greeting.

Bellamy nodded, then glanced over at Jessa. She was meant to be guarding him, but instead the two of them had been trying to figure out a way to enact his plan. Jessa gave the area a quick scan, listening for voices—Paul, Clarke, or Vale—approaching. Satisfied they were alone, she beckoned toward Luke, who tiptoed over and crouched next to Bellamy.

"How you bearing up?" Luke whispered.

"Oh, I'm just great." Bellamy tried for a shrug, but his arms wouldn't move that far. "This is how I spend all my Saturdays."

Luke grinned briefly before his face fell serious again.

Bellamy swallowed. "Did you find it?"

"I did," Luke said, his eyes flashing bright.

Bellamy sat up a little, wincing from the pain in his back. Luke reached out to help adjust him, but Bellamy shook his head, handling it himself.

"I left just after Cooper and Vale," Luke went on in a

whisper. "Felix relieved me at my post and told Paul I'd gone to rest in the campsite. Cooper and Vale didn't notice me trailing them. I waited until Cooper caught the raiders' attention and then I went to where you told me. I found the ammunitions store quickly . . . maybe too quickly. Bellamy, they're bound to notice it's caved open soon."

"I know," Bellamy said darkly. "Did you go in?"

"I thought I'd wait for you," Luke said with a smirk. "I'd hate for you to miss all the fun."

"Okay," Bellamy said, the gears in his mind finally starting to whir back to life. "Who's guarding me tonight?"

"If it's not Jessa, we'll make sure it's Jessa," Luke said.

At the mention of her name, Jessa glanced casually over her shoulder, flashing a quick blink of acknowledgment. Bellamy smiled grimly back.

"We'd let you go now, man, if we didn't think it would sabotage the rest of our plans." Luke sighed.

"I know," Bellamy said quickly. "I wouldn't want you to. And anyway, free range of arm motion is hugely overrated."

"You'll need to limber up fast once we spring you tonight, though," Luke said dryly. "We'll need every set of arms we can get."

"Who *have* we got?"

"Me, you, and Felix," Luke said. "Jessa's going to stay behind to keep them from stopping us."

"Why would they care?" Bellamy asked. "We're not going to interfere with the negotiations. This is just a . . . backup plan."

He heard low voices behind them again, over the wall in the campsite. Paul was offering Clarke food, cracking jokes about his foraging skills, and she kept trying to change the subject back to next steps.

Next steps. Diplomacy.

Bellamy swallowed around a pit in his throat.

They weren't doing *nothing*, exactly, were they? Plan A was moving forward. Clarke still held out hope for a peaceful resolution. Was she right? Was he being reckless, after all?

Sensing him waver, Luke leaned forward. "We've got a good shot here. And a really short window for it."

Bellamy shook his head, thinking. "Cooper got inside, though, unharmed. Vale said so."

Luke snorted. "That just means these bastards have one more of us locked inside their compound."

"But what if it means more than that? What if "—Bellamy nodded behind him, unable to say her name—"their plan is working?"

"Then we'll still have taken away all the munitions in the meantime. We'll have an even greater advantage . . . a bargaining chip. Win-win, right?"

"Right." Bellamy frowned. It was strange. The whole journey here, he'd pictured Octavia's and Wells's faces as clearly as if they were standing right in front of him, begging him for help. But now that he had a plan, all he could see was Clarke, the hurt in her eyes last night, the expression on her face when he drove her away.

He imagined something even worse now: the look she would have tonight when she realized he was gone. The realization that, in the end, he'd betrayed her for what might be the final time without even bothering to say good-bye.

He closed his eyes, sorrow welling in his chest. He'd been wrong to accuse her of not caring. Even more wrong to think of her as a coward. Clarke would always be one of the fiercest people he'd ever known, and here she was, standing up for what she thought was right.

"Listen, man," Luke was saying to him, rocking back onto his heels with a heavy sigh. "If you're getting cold feet, if you don't think this is the right thing . . ."

Bellamy opened his mouth to answer, but before he could, Luke let out a frustrated huff, his fists balling by his sides.

"No, screw that." Luke shook his head. "I'm sorry, Bel, I am, but your plan is the best one we've got. And *Glass* is in there." His cheeks grew mottled, his red-rimmed eyes welling fast. "She's *in there.* I've got to get her out."

Bellamy watched him for a moment, his thoughts swirling and landing and settling at last on something that felt like a final answer. "No cold feet, Luke."

Luke's eyes locked on his.

Bellamy nodded back—a promise.

"This happens tonight."

CHAPTER *23*

Glass

Glass held tight to the skirt of her white dress, willing her smile to stay steady as she strolled with Soren along a corridor with cracked walls covered in ivy and roses. The first time Glass had seen the flowers, a few days earlier, she'd marveled at how lovely they looked against the crumbling concrete. Beauty triumphing over ugliness. Nature redeeming the sins of the humans who'd taken her for granted. But now the roses just looked *trapped*, far from the woods and meadows where they belonged.

"It's a lovely ceremony," the High Protector was explaining, the midday light filtering through the ruined ceiling hitting her face in disorienting flashes. "The first ritual will be held outdoors at sunrise tomorrow. The men and women are washed and anointed and blessed by Earth Herself before the actual pairing begins."

"I'm sorry," Glass said. "I think I'm still a little confused. What exactly goes on at the Pairing Ceremony?"

"Oh, goodness, *yes*." Soren laughed and it sounded like sunshine. "Of course you're curious. It's when the new recruits, girls like you that Earth has gifted us, become true members of our community. We pair each new girl with one of the male recruits, and they consummate the union, thereby becoming Protectors. Then, if their pairing pleases Earth, She blesses us with a true-born child."

Glass stumbled and held on to the wall while she tried to blink her dizziness away. "Consummate?" she whispered.

Surely Soren couldn't mean what Glass thought she was implying. Was the Pairing Ceremony a mating ritual? Was that why Glass and the other girls had been taken? A memory slithered out from the back of her brain. Luke's roommate, Carter, placing his hands on her waist, trapping her against the wall. The feel of his warm breath too close to her skin. She squeezed her eyes shut, fighting back waves of nausea.

"Yes," Soren said. "As I'd told you, the Pairing Ceremony dates back to the very first Protectors, and the outsiders who welcomed them in. Most of those Protectors healed from the radiation they'd been exposed to on the surface. Outwardly, anyway. When it came time to bring a new generation into the world, they found that they were unable to conceive . . ." She trailed off and looked at Glass, as if prompting her to continue the story.

A chill ran down Glass's spine and she scrambled to connect the dots. "They had the new people conceive for them," she said slowly as unsettling images filled her head.

Soren nodded. "Exactly. The following generations didn't have the same problems, but it became the most honored ritual in our society, and we've been doing it ever since. New recruits are always a little nervous, of course, as I'm sure brides and grooms were in the old world, but with everyone taking part together, it adds a level of unity and community that's hard to describe."

Glass's mouth fell open as her stomach roiled. There was no way Soren could mean . . . right there, in the open, with everyone watching. *That* was how they would all prove themselves invaluable to the community?

No. She couldn't let this happen. Her heart beat frantically against her rib cage, a trapped bird begging for escape. *Luke.* He had to be on his way to find her. He'd never let this happen to her. He'd find a way . . .

"I normally arrange the pairs, of course," Soren said. "But you're so special to me, and it's important to me that you feel comfortable. So I was wondering, would you like to be paired with that friend of yours? The handsome dark-haired one?"

"Wells?" Glass asked hoarsely, her throat suddenly dry.

"Yes, he shows a lot of promise, my men tell me."

Oh my god. Oh my god. The corridor started to spin as gut-wrenching images flooded her head. Wells's face burning with shame as he looked away, trying to afford his childhood friend a shred of dignity as she undressed in front of him. The agony in his eyes as he was forced to . . . whispering, "I'm so sorry, Glass," while he . . .

No. It was too terrible to imagine.

Though not nearly as terrible as the image of the girls in the den being shoved into the arms of leering strangers. Lina. Anna. *Octavia.*

Soren glanced behind her as they neared the sprawling courtyard at the center of the building. "I think we'll perform the ritual here, Glass. The Heart of the Stone. What better place?"

Glass struggled to breathe. Every time she tried to inhale, the breath caught in her chest. Finally, she managed to wheeze out, "That all sounds great."

Soren pressed her hands into Glass's shoulders, pleased. "I'm touched, Glass. I can tell how much this means to you. Would you like to be the one to tell your friends about the honor that awaits them? I'm sure it'll mean a great deal, coming from you."

"Yes," Glass said, taking one last shaky breath.

"Wonderful." Soren sniffed, her tone returning to all-business briskness. "Now's as good a time as any. I've got something to attend to at the front gates." Her face clouded. "Something . . . unpleasant, I'm afraid. I'll look forward to picking up our chat where we left off when I get back."

She smiled gratefully, reaching out to clasp Glass's hand one more time before turning and striding purposefully away down a southern corridor, the word *unpleasant* seeming to linger in the air behind her like a noxious cloud.

Glass shuddered and turned to walk quickly to the sculleries. As much as she dreaded this, it was much better that they found out as quickly as possible. There had to be a way they could get out of it . . .

She turned a corner, passing the lines of hung laundry, half of it seemingly abandoned, baskets heaped with wet linens, then poked her head inside the steaming scullery. A quick glance showed Lina scrubbing chamber pots along with a few other girls, cloths tied tight over their disgusted faces, but no one else familiar.

A giggle echoed down the alley behind her. She spun around, following the sound to a little bombed-out niche in the massive wall, where two girls stood tangled up in each other. Octavia's hands were loosening Anna's curly braid, Anna's fingers dancing up Octavia's spine . . . and they were kissing like it was the greatest discovery of their lifetimes.

In any other situation, seeing Octavia look so happy would've filled Glass's heart with joy. But right now, all she could see was the upcoming Pairing Ceremony. Anna forced to watch as Octavia was shoved into a strange man's arms . . . a man whom Earth had "willed" to do what he liked with her.

Stomach churning, Glass cleared her throat.

Anna and Octavia broke apart with a lurch, terror mirrored on each of their faces until they saw who was standing in front of them, and they doubled over with relief and a wonderfully mundane kind of embarrassment.

"We need to talk," Glass said. "Quickly."

Both girls went pale as Glass recited the whole sordid plan: the pairings, the ceremony, officially being inducted as Protectors. She kept her gaze cast down at the rocky floor, too horrified by Soren's intentions to even look them in the eye as she told them.

When she was done, she glanced up at Octavia, and to her surprise, saw more determination than fear in the younger girl's face.

"It's time, Glass," Octavia said. "You know it is."

"Wells hasn't signaled that it's time yet."

Octavia gripped Glass's wrist. "No. You have to kill her. You're the only one close enough to do it."

"I . . ." Glass felt bile rising in her throat. She was disgusted by the Protectors, but *kill* Soren? She looked to Anna, but Anna was staring at her feet. Glass swallowed. "I think that would raise too many alarms. We just need to get our people out. That's the only priority."

Octavia's hand slid from Glass's wrist, her face falling.

Glass stepped forward. "Have you thought any more about your river plan and using the boats to escape?"

Octavia nodded. "As long as we can manufacture some kind of distraction, we'll be able to row far enough away that we'll be out of gunshot range. They could take a wagon and try to catch up, but there's no road along the river. I think we'll make it."

"We need to find Wells and let him know what's happening. We need to escape tonight, before the

Pairing Ceremony happens tomorrow morning. Can you find him?" Glass asked.

"Don't worry." Octavia's voice was firm. "I'll figure something out."

Looking at the fierceness in her eyes, Glass believed her. After everything they'd been through, everything they'd survived, none of them were going down without a fight.

CHAPTER *24*

Wells

When they'd gotten back to the Stone that morning, Wells had dragged Graham off to the kennels, just as he'd been asked to do. But clearly Graham's insubordination had put the Protectors on alert, because they immediately whisked Wells to a cramped, isolated room. They'd slammed the door and left him in there for hours. Based on the hunger rumbling in his stomach, it was at least late afternoon by now.

Sitting in the dark, alone for the first time since they'd arrived four days ago, Wells had finally come to a realization: They couldn't afford to wait for the right time to escape. There would never be a right time. These people were unpredictable, and that's what made them so dangerous. He had to talk to the other recruits, the people who had been captured from other places, and try to convince some of them to rise up against the Protectors with them. It was their best chance. It was their *only* chance.

Now he just needed to get out of this damn room.

His eyes had adjusted to the darkness, so it was painful when the door finally creaked open and Oak walked in, holding a lantern.

He'd seen hatred on Oak's face before. He knew it well, that paper-thin veneer of calm the Protector wore, covering a deep well of violence underneath. But the way Oak was staring at the ground right now was the most frightening expression Wells had ever seen. With the lantern light flickering on his hollowed-out face, Oak looked more demon than man.

"We wanted you to be a Protector," Oak growled, his voice low and dangerous. "We wanted to trust you and welcome you into our fold."

"I had nothing to do with what Graham did," Wells said, willing his voice steady. "You have to know that I'm—"

Oak lunged for him, closing the distance between them in one great stride, and gripped Wells's throat with a hand as rough and relentless as a hangman's noose. Wells saw spots and fought to breathe. The lantern light in front of him started to fade out, his vision blurring. With his remaining ounce of strength, he kicked his legs out, trying to free himself from Oak's grasp.

The door behind them clanged open and Oak released him suddenly. Wells fell to the ground and tumbled over, gripping his own throat and desperately sucking in air with tight, rasping breaths.

"It's all right," a woman's voice soothed from a few feet away. "No harm done."

Wells looked up, thinking the words were directed at him, but blinked hard at the strange sight of Oak kneeling before the High Protector. Soren was stroking the old man's head like a dog, and he had his eyes closed.

"You may go," she told Oak, and the Protector rose and left the room in one smooth, silent movement. He didn't seem to give Soren's order even a millisecond of thought; he just obeyed it.

Soren picked up the lantern Oak had discarded. Where the candle's flame had rendered Oak demonic, it made the High Protector look serene and angelic. But he reminded himself to remain on his guard. *She's worse than any of them*, Wells reminded himself. *She's the one pulling all the strings*.

"I'm sorry for that," Soren said, lowering herself to sit before him, her legs crossed under her long skirts.

"Everyone's a little rattled today. We've had . . . a visitor, you see, at the front gates. An unexpected one."

Wells froze, his heart racing. Had their friends come for them?

"And then your raiding party returned and we learned what had happened." She shook her head sadly. "It's tipped them over the edge, I'm afraid."

"What Graham did is inexcusable," Wells said hoarsely, his throat still aching from Oak's attack.

Soren gave him a tight smile. "I'm inclined to agree. *And* I'm inclined to believe that you had nothing to do with it."

She reached out and gently clasped his wrist. "I have plans for you, Wells," she said, her eyes sparkling.

Wells fought the sudden impulse to pull his arm away from her, as if he was recoiling from a snake that had just reared its venomous head. *Plans* meant that she expected him to stay here for the long-term.

Play along, he reminded himself. *Just long enough to stay alive.*

"These plans are for the faithful. For Earth and for *us*." She squeezed his wrist tighter. "So tell me. Are you one of us?"

"Yes," he said, as firmly as he could manage while his mind whirred. What could he say to convince her? "I was just as shocked as everybody else by what Graham did. I just wish I'd been able to warn you about him sooner."

Soren leaned back and surveyed him carefully. "What do you mean?"

Wells clenched his jaw. "I've been wary of Graham for a very long time. He was on the dropship that brought me down to Earth." He nodded reverently downward, the way the Protectors always did when referencing Earth incidentally. "I learned very quickly not to trust him. I don't even think it's about him not accepting Earth's wisdom. I think he *has*. I just think he's unstable and needs . . ."

The door opened behind Soren. She cocked her head without turning as her blond advisor stepped inside, pulling a limp figure behind her. *Graham.*

"He's awake," the advisor said.

Wells bit his lip to stop himself from gasping as the blond woman yanked Graham into the room and let him fall to the floor. He *was* awake, though you could hardly tell. His head, puffy and caked with blood, lolled against the wall where she'd left him. His eyes traveled to Wells's, completely expressionless, as the woman in gray stepped out again, shutting the door behind her.

Soren touched Wells's knee, her sweet smile never wavering. "You were saying?"

Wells glanced at Graham, swallowing hard. Graham kept staring, as though he didn't have enough energy to blink. Only the rise and fall of his chest told Wells that he was even alive.

Wells looked at Soren. "I think he's . . . unwell. Mentally. From the moment we landed, he did everything he could to undermine my standing in our camp, for no other reason but petty rivalry. He drew a line in the sand on our very first day on Earth and put my life and the lives of my friends in danger every single chance he could get. So if you're asking if I'm with *him* . . ." He contorted his face into a sneer. "The answer is no."

Graham's gaze dipped slowly down to the floor, Wells's stomach sinking with it. He had to be so careful. If they thought he was in league with Graham, any hope of escaping with their friends would be lost. But he couldn't risk making too convincing a case that Graham was irredeemable either. He couldn't put Graham at any more risk than he already was.

Wells swallowed.

"I'm sorry, Mother," Wells said, shaking his head.

Her eyes widened, a quick flash, barely perceptible. "For what, Wells?"

"For dwelling on the past. I was meant to have washed it all away in the river, I know that. Whatever happened before is gone now." He peered up at her. "This is my home now, if Earth wills it."

"If Earth wills it," she repeated, her voice hushed, continuing to watch him.

Just as he was losing all hope that she'd bought that sudden display of devotion, she leaned over and kissed his forehead.

"I believe you," she said. "And at dawn tomorrow, I'll be performing what we call the Pairing Ceremony with you and the other recruits, where we officially welcome you into our fold as Protectors."

She pulled a dagger out of a pocket in her long, flowing skirts. It glinted dangerously in the low light of the room. Wells held his breath, heart racing, as Soren ran its blade along the inside of Wells's arm, then sliced through the ropes binding him.

Wells let out a long sigh of relief, rotating his ankles and wrists until the feeling returned to them in sharp prickles. Pocketing her dagger, Soren stood.

"The others will require more, of course," she went on. "My Protectors." Soren pressed her hand to her heart, smiling indulgently, like she was talking about small children. "Our community's very existence requires our men to be brutes. It's what they know, and it's what they respect. If you want to join our community and be accepted by them, they're going to need a *brutal* kind of proof from you. It's the only way to get them to trust you."

Wells felt his breath stilling, icy in his chest.

"Take this young man out to the forest and kill him," she ordered, her voice light as ever. "You can make it as quick or as drawn out as you like, but do it well outside our sacred walls, please. We don't need any more blood spilled here today."

No. The word tore through Wells as hatred and revulsion battled for dominance. This was where it ended. They had to get out of here. *Now.* A second wave of nausea crashed over him as the implications of Soren's words sank in. What did she mean by *more blood*? His mind raced back to that mention she'd made of an unexpected visitor. Now he prayed with every fiber of his being that it *hadn't* been one of his friends.

"Oak will accompany you as a witness to your obedient service." Soren opened the door and waved Oak over, then glided away without another look back.

Oak filled the doorframe, two guns clutched in his ropy hands. He trained them on Graham. Graham stood shakily and walked out the door, like one of the Earthborns' sheep being herded to its pasture.

Graham glanced over at Wells, but Wells couldn't read any expression through his swollen eyes and bruised jaw.

The sky was starting to darken toward sunset. They walked in silence out of the small front entrance to the

Stone, picking their way through the courtyard, into the forest beyond. As they reached the line of trees, Wells swore he could see something strange out of the corner of his eye, a bright flame moving westward fast, but he didn't dare turn for fear of giving Oak an excuse to pull the trigger.

Every time Wells thought they might stop—this had to have been far enough—they would keep going, dread gripping him tighter and tighter with every step.

Finally, Oak barked, "Here," and Graham and Wells stopped walking.

Wells turned slowly, arms high, then winced as Oak shoved one of the guns across his chest. Oak stared at him expectantly, and Wells grasped for a way to buy time. He'd find a way out of this nightmare. He had to.

"Can I—can I have a moment alone with Graham to say good-bye?"

Oak's eyes softened slightly. "Fine, but I'll be right over there if you need me." He pointed to the perimeter of the Stone, then turned to walk away.

Wells held his breath, his pulse stilling to a cold, steady beat. What could he do? He could either kill Graham, or refuse and be killed himself, or kill Oak. There wasn't an option. He lifted the barrel of the gun and trained it at

Oak's retreating back. He closed one eye, taking aim, his finger on the trigger and—

Two bound hands pulled the barrel down again.

Wells gasped, turning to Graham, whispering, "What are you doing?" He wrestled the rifle free. "We'll shoot him and we'll run."

Graham smiled bleakly. His eyes were so swollen with bruises that Wells could barely see his eyes. "You really think it's that simple? I can barely walk after what they did to me. How are we going to get away? They'd come after us, and they'd kill us *both*. I'm a dead man either way. But you can get back in there and help our people. And if you can bring these bastards down in the process, so much the better."

Wells wiped sweat from his forehead. "What are you saying?"

"You know what I'm saying, Jaha, don't be obtuse."

"There's another way—" Wells's breaths came short, frantic. "I'll fire at the tree. Give you a chance to run, say I missed."

"They'll kill you for missing."

"I'll dig a hole and say I buried you, I'll—"

"They'll want to see a body, Wells, *think*!" Graham's whisper rose into a shout. He sucked his voice back in, shaking his head, his eyes growing distant. "All those things you said in there . . ."

Wells's mouth went dry, though he kept his gun trained on Graham so Oak wouldn't get suspicious. "Graham. I didn't—"

"They were *true*." His eyes rose to meet Wells's, wide and clear. "I am not a good person. I'm not. Never have been, not for my entire life. But *you* are." Graham snorted. "I think it's what's always bugged me the most about you."

"I . . ." Wells's head slumped. Graham was wrong—it had been a very long time since he'd considered himself a good person by any definition of the word. But this, what they were asking him to do, was a new level of monstrous. "I won't do this. I can't."

"Sure you can," Graham said, a slight tremor in his whisper betraying the fear underneath it. "I'm giving you permission. Your conscience is totally clear."

Wells's hands were slick with sweat against the cold metal of the gun. He glanced down at it, and then back up at the other boy. Graham's cheeks were wet with tears.

"I never told you what I did back on the ship, did I?" Graham asked, his whisper cracking like a bad radio signal. "What they confined me for?"

Wells watched wordlessly as Graham raised his

eyebrows and fell to his knees, until he was peering up at Wells through the darkness, his jaw set and eyes streaming.

"I've done bad things, Jaha. You don't even know how many bad things. *Let me do this one noble thing now.* Please. *Please* just let me."

Wells could hardly look at Graham, his longtime enemy's forehead contorted with pain as he pleaded . . . not for his life, but for his own *death*. There was no trace here of the smirking, strutting Phoenician boy Wells knew. That Graham was already gone.

But *this* one was well worth saving.

"No," Wells said, certainty cementing in his muscles. "We'll find another wa—"

Graham's hand darted out for Wells's trigger before he could so much as blink. The blast rang out through the forest, through the air, through Wells's head and heart and bones.

He stared at the smoking barrel, and then at the spot where Graham had been kneeling, and then, last and longest, at Graham's lifeless crumpled body, his blood pouring in rivulets over the blanket of leaves beneath him.

Thoughts broke through the cloud of horror surrounding Wells.

Graham could have run. He could have been selfish. Anybody would have in his position.

He died to save us.

Minutes, hours, days passed, Wells hardly knew . . . and then a hand gripped his shoulder. Wells flinched, closed his eyes, and turned to see Oak staring at him with solemn pride.

"You've learned," the Protector said. "Well done, son. Let's go home."

CHAPTER 25

Bellamy

It felt amazing to be roaming through the woods again. Jumping lightly over fallen logs, taking care to stay in the shadows of the trees, Bellamy could almost pretend he was out on another hunting trip. Even Luke's presence next to him felt familiar. As his leg started to heal, he'd begun to join Bellamy on some of his outings. Normally, Bellamy resented having someone with him—most people moved slowly, or loudly, or felt the need to fill the silence with mindless chatter. Yet Luke was content to spend hours in the woods barely exchanging a word, communicating with just the odd nod or hand gesture when one of them spotted a target.

But he and Luke weren't looking for a deer to bring back to camp. They were about to sneak into a fortress full of weird, white-clad murderers and steal their bombs.

"We're getting close, right?" Luke asked quietly, finally breaking the silence. "This all looks a little different to me in the dark."

"Yes. The entrance Felix and I found is just through those trees." He pointed to a spot where the trees thinned out, revealing glimpses of a crumbling concrete wall.

As they got closer, they both grew quieter, until they were moving silently across the damp leaf-covered forest floor. He motioned for Luke to take cover behind one of the trees nearest the wall, and he did the same. For a long moment, they stood there, straining their ears for any sign of activity. But nothing came.

Bellamy crept forward, taking a few steps onto the grass path that formed a narrow perimeter around the five-sided fortress. He turned from side to side, and when he was sure the coast was clear, he beckoned for Luke to join him.

The air buzzed with an electricity Bellamy couldn't quite identify, as if, at any moment, a sea of white-clad men with shaved heads would flood out of a hidden door, bullets flying. Yet as they hurried along the wall, nothing disturbed the silence except the sound of their own breath.

A few moments later, he found it—the hole in the ground that led straight down into their armory, or whatever the hell those cretins called it. After he and Felix had discovered it the other night, they'd covered the hole up with some debris—planks and rocks that were strewn about the field—to keep light from streaming inside. That was probably why none of their guards had noticed it. It never would've escaped Bellamy's eye, though. He never overlooked any detail that could possibly signal danger. He couldn't help it. It was in his DNA. It's what kept him and his sister alive all those years they were in hiding. *That's* why he'd noticed the strange pile of leaves, the one Clarke had dismissed.

If only she'd listened to him. If only he'd trusted *himself* enough to make her listen.

Gently, Bellamy picked up some of the planks and pushed them aside. Then he got down on his knees and put his ear to the ground. There were no sounds coming from below; the armory was empty. He lowered himself into the cellar. Then he blinked, trying to force his eyes to adjust to the dim light as quickly as possible.

By the time Luke was scrambling to his feet next to him, the shadowy shapes were coming into focus. There was the cart that he'd spotted the other night, still full of weapons. Guns, knives . . . and grenades.

"You ready?" Bellamy asked Luke. Luke nodded solemnly.

They'd planned this out in advance. There was one cart's worth of supplies, and if they worked quickly, they could take it all. Bellamy and Luke had brought empty sacks with them from their campsite and carefully filled them up. Then they pulled themselves out of the hole in the ground and ran quietly back to the woods.

In the forest, they emptied out the sacks, hiding the weapons underneath the brush, then hurried back to the armory for more. They did this four times, as stealthily as they could in order to avoid detection, until there were only a few weapons left.

On their last trip in, as they loaded up their bags, a faint, melodic sound drifted toward them. Both Luke and Bellamy froze, like the deer sometimes did when they spotted Bellamy with his bow drawn, arrow locked in place. Someone was *singing*.

Let's go, Luke mouthed, starting to inch back toward the opening.

But Bellamy felt himself being pulled the other way, toward the warped metal door that was too bent to close properly, light streaming through the gaps. Silently, he crept up to the door and peered out.

Two girls with braided hair and white tunics were

walking down a hallway, singing while they carried a large silver platter between them.

When Earth was just a maiden fair
A goddess with white clouds for hair
She wished upon the stars above
For a child She could fill with love

Their strangely blank expressions and oddly harmonious voices sent chills down Bellamy's spine. What the hell was going on here? But as the girls came closer, his uneasiness turned to alarm. He *knew* one of them. It was Lina, the Earthborn girl from Max's village. One of the people who'd been taken.

He willed her to glance at the door so he could motion to her. If he could only catch her attention, he could get her out of there. But she continued to stare straight ahead, her eyes wide and unfocused.

As they drifted past, a short, scowling man stormed into the corridor. "What took you so long? The Protectors are waiting for their dinner," he snapped.

The second girl smiled. "The kitchen is far from the barracks," she said dreamily.

"Well, try to speed it up next time."

"If Earth wills it," the girl said.

"If Earth wills it," Lina echoed.

What the . . .

Bellamy turned away, scooped up his bag, then nodded at Luke and crawled back through the hole. When he stood up, blinking in the moonlight, he found that he was shaking.

"What happened?" Luke asked. "What did you see in there?"

"I saw Lina," Bellamy said breathlessly as they both hurried back into the safety of the woods. "You know, the Earthborn girl."

Luke's eyes widened. "Was she okay? Was anyone else with her? Did you see any sign of Glass?"

"She was with another girl I didn't recognize, but, Luke, there is something really, really strange going on there. I think . . ." He paused, not wanting to say the words aloud, afraid of what it'd mean for Octavia and the others. "I think they've been brainwashed."

He explained what he'd seen, watching Luke's jaw tighten and his eyes narrow.

"Thank goodness they're alive, though. We'll get them out of there," Luke said quietly. "No matter what it takes." He clenched and unclenched his fists. "Did you get any sense of the layout?"

"I'm pretty sure the armory is next to the guards'

barracks. The girls were bringing food in from the kitchen, which they said was far away."

"Okay . . . okay . . . that's good," Luke said. "We know what area to hit if we need to." He let out a long breath, as if he'd been holding it for a while. "Should we go tell the others?"

Bellamy hoisted his grenade-filled bag over his shoulder. Suddenly, confronting Clarke and Paul seemed like child's play compared to what they would have to do afterward. "Let's go."

CHAPTER 26

Clarke

The forest was so quiet, it felt as though it was holding its breath.

It had only been an hour since Clarke had relieved Felix and taken his place at the lookout point. But each minute was piling onto the next like a weight bearing down on her, heavier and heavier. Cooper should've been back by now. It shouldn't have taken the whole day for him to talk to the raiders.

She didn't want to think about the possibility, but maybe it had all gone wrong.

Clarke stretched as best she could, without creeping too far out of position, trying to wring the thick worry out of her limbs. There was no sense in panicking. She would just have to wait and hope.

A twig cracked behind her. Clarke glanced quickly back. There was no one there. She took a deep breath, trying to quiet her racing heart. She wasn't doing anyone any good by waiting here. It would make more sense for her to go look for Cooper, in case he needed backup. Whatever that meant in this case.

She crept toward the edge of the forest that bordered the fortress, wondering whether to ignore the prickle on the back of her neck. Bellamy had had feelings like that, and his instincts turned out to be right. But Clarke wasn't like that. Her whole life had been about learning to trust her brain instead of her heart. That's what they'd taught her during her medical training. That's what her parents had impressed on her when she'd confronted them about their gruesome experiments. She had to think in terms of the "big picture" and the "larger good," even when her gut was shouting something far different.

It grew brighter as she approached the edge of the forest, and the trees cast long, strange shadows in the moonlight. A shape emerged, the silhouette of a person. Clarke's breath caught in her chest and she froze, unsure whether to dash for a tree or stay perfectly still.

She waited. She didn't breathe.

The figure didn't move.

Her heart was beating so fast, she was sure whoever was out there could hear. Still the figure didn't move. But whoever it was had to have spotted her. There was no point in trying to hide.

"Cooper," she called hoarsely. "Is that you?" Once the echo of her voice faded, there was only silence.

Slowly, she walked forward. "Cooper?" she tried again. "Are you okay?"

As she moved closer, Clarke realized that it wasn't Cooper. It wasn't anyone, really. She squinted, wondering if her eyes were deceiving her. But, no . . . she could see it clearly—the loose clothes stuffed with straw, the crude human features on the gourd head—it was a scarecrow, a thing she'd once read about.

Normally, encountering pre-Cataclysm artifacts filled her with excitement and wonder, but not this time. Something was wrong. They were too far from any crops for this to be a *new* scarecrow, and there was no way an old one could've survived the Cataclysm.

A few meters away, Clarke froze. *No* . . . she blinked . . . it had to be a trick of the light.

"No," she breathed. "No, please."

It wasn't a scarecrow. Not entirely. Because, while the

loose clothes were indeed filled with straw, the head wasn't made from a gourd like she'd first thought.

It was a real human head.

Cooper's.

Clarke screamed. She couldn't stop it. Her shrieks rang up into the trees, sending two birds flapping away wildly. "Help!" she shouted. "Someone, please, help!" And then before she knew what she was doing, a name burst out of her throat. "Bellamy!"

She gasped, her head spinning, but then her initial wave of terror and revulsion receded, and her training kicked in. She staggered forward, steeling herself for what awaited. Cooper's head had been severed and placed on a spike, on which someone had also affixed the body of a scarecrow— straw stuffed into Cooper's clothes.

His face was round and bloated, his skin a stomach-churning blue. But the blood near the neck stem was still wet. This had happened recently. Clarke scanned the shadows for signs of movement. She took a deep breath and slowly walked around the gruesome effigy, then let out another gasp.

On the scarecrow's back were written the words *Serve or die*. And they'd been written in blood.

"Oh shit," someone whispered. Clarke spun around

and saw Paul staring at the scarecrow, his face white with horror.

"I know . . ." Clarke said, forcing herself to breathe as tears began to fall down her cheeks. "We should look for the body. We can't leave him like this."

"What? No way," Paul said, backing away.

"Okay, fine, I'll deal with it later. But we need to figure out what to do next."

But Paul had already turned around and was breaking into a run.

"Hey!" Clarke called. "Where are you going?"

A crashing sound made Clarke jump to the side. She grabbed a stick from the ground and raised it above her head, ready to pummel whoever emerged from the trees.

"Clarke! Are you okay? I'm coming! Clarke!"

She dropped the stick as Bellamy sprinted out of the shadows. When he saw her, his red, sweat-covered face collapsed with relief and he pulled her into a tight embrace. "I heard you scream and I thought . . ." His words were drowned out by a sound that was half laugh, half sob. "Thank god you're all right."

A few moments later, Luke emerged, moving smartly despite his limp, and dragging Paul with him.

"What's going on?" Bellamy snarled, turning to Paul. "What did you do to her?"

"I didn't do anything. *They* did *that*." He gestured wildly at the scarecrow.

Bellamy spun around, seeing it for the first time. "Oh my god," he muttered, taking a few shaky steps backward. "Holy shit."

"Let go of me, you idiot." Paul groaned as he tried to free himself from Luke's grasp. "I had nothing to do with this."

"Then why were you running away?" Luke said through gritted teeth, tightening his hold until Paul let out a whimper.

"Because it'd be insane to stick around here. Look what they did to Cooper! We have no chance in hell of rescuing anyone. It's time to get out."

"You want to abandon them?" Clarke said, unable to keep the disdain out of her voice. Bellamy shot her a look of pride for standing up to Paul.

"Yes. We are out of our freaking depth here. My thoughts and prayers go out to our people on the inside, et cetera, et cetera, but we are *marching home right now*."

"You can go," Bellamy said, wrapping his arm around Clarke. "But the rest of us are staying. We have work to do."

Bellamy and Clarke walked a little behind Luke, who was dragging along a whining, whimpering Paul. "Are you sure you're okay?" Bellamy asked, glancing back over his shoulder. "What you saw . . . what they did to Cooper . . ."

"I'm okay," Clarke said, though the quaver in her voice suggested otherwise. "After we tell the others, I'll go back and tend to the . . ." She trailed off before she could say the word *body*.

Bellamy tightened his hold. "I'll go with you. We'll do it together." Even with her medical training, the thought of the morbid task made her slightly woozy, and Clarke leaned against him, knowing he'd never let her fall.

"I'm so sorry," she said softly. "I can't believe I let Paul do that to you. I'll never forgive myself."

Bellamy didn't respond, but he didn't loosen his grip around her either. When he finally spoke, his voice was quiet and measured. "I know you won't. That's why I'm sorry about the terrible things I said. You carry so much pain with you, Clarke. And I used that against you. I knew how to hurt you, and I went for it. Can you forgive me?"

She knew he was right, but hearing the tenderness in his voice was enough to make that weight disappear, if only for a moment. "Yes, if you can forgive me."

He let out a long sigh. "I haven't really been myself lately. You were right to be cautious."

She stopped walking and turned to look up at him. "I love all of you, Bellamy Blake."

He smiled and kissed the top of her head. "I love you," he whispered into her hair.

The others were waiting anxiously for them when they returned. Clarke told them about Cooper, and then went to hold a shaking Vale, who'd collapsed into tears.

"He didn't have to come," Vale said in between sobs. "He volunteered because that's the kind of person he is . . . was . . ."

"And we're sure as hell going to make sure he didn't die in vain," Bellamy said, pacing over to some bags by the fire. "We're going to rescue our people, and then we're going to make the bastards pay. For Cooper. For our camp. For god knows what else they've destroyed, and think they can get away with it." He reached into one of the bags and pulled out a gun.

"We got them from our enemy's armory," Luke explained to Clarke. "We emptied the whole thing out. We carried what we could here, before we heard you scream, and we hid the rest of it in the woods. I also had the opportunity to look at the structure itself. It looks impregnable from a distance, but when you get close, you discover fissures running all along the foundations, probably caused by the blasts from the Cataclysm and natural erosion over time. All it would take is careful placement of even a handful of these explosives and those outer walls would come tumbling down."

Luke nodded to Bellamy. He stepped forward and picked up the thread.

"During the chaos, the raiders will run for their arsenal—and they'll find it emptied out. Some of them will already have weapons on hand, of course. We'll focus on those people, disarm them first, then head to the armory, where the rest of them will be gathered together in a tight space."

"Sitting ducks," Felix said, smiling weakly.

Clarke's heart clenched a little. Bellamy had used those same words when he'd confronted Clarke about his suspicions before the Harvest Feast. He must've sensed her pain, because he lowered his gun and walked over to take her hand.

"Once they've been neutralized, we'll find our friends and lead them home," he went on. "Maybe we'll even take back some of the food and supplies they stole from us on the way out."

Paul snorted. "Three problems. This is a sophisticated enemy, their fortress is a death trap, and . . . oh yeah, you're all going to *die*."

"Funny how you keep saying *you* like you're not coming with us," Jessa said, nudging her gun at him. Paul's face went bone white.

"Clarke, you know this is insane, right?" Paul looked at her imploringly.

"Well," she said slowly. "It's brash and reckless and a little bit impulsive . . ." Bellamy started to flush slightly. "But it's also clever and brave. All the things I love most." She smiled at him. "Lead the way, Councilor."

CHAPTER *27*

Wells

As Wells walked through the halls of the Stone, the Protectors looked at him, their heads turning in a slow wave. But instead of suspicion, their eyes shone with approval.

Word had traveled fast. Oak had made sure of it. Anger pulsed through Wells's veins.

On their way back to the barracks, Oak steered Wells into the mess hall. "Dinner's over, but Soren knows you missed your meal, so we've saved some for you."

Wells was surprised to see Octavia waiting for them there, carrying a silver platter. "I was sent to bring food to . . ." She nodded toward Wells.

"Eat, son," Oak said, guiding him to a table. He patted Wells on the back and then ambled off to go talk to a few Protectors in the corner of the room, giving Wells and Octavia a blessed moment of alone time—another sign that they trusted him.

"Glass asked me to find you," Octavia said quickly and quietly, glancing to the corner. No one was watching them. "She found some things out about this Pairing Ceremony. It's bad, Wells. We need to get out of here. I hate to admit it, but I'm—I'm scared."

"I know," Wells said. "These people are monsters. But look, I have a plan. They're going to put all of the recruits together for the Pairing Ceremony, right?"

Octavia nodded, slowly placing his meal in front of him. "Right. Glass said we'd be in the Heart of the Stone."

"But not all of the actual Protectors will be there," Wells continued. "Some will have to be guarding the building. So I'd bet there are going to be more recruits than Protectors present at the ceremony."

Octavia cast her gaze around the room. "You're saying . . . you think we'll outnumber them?"

Wells nodded. "I'm betting on it. If we can convince all the other recruits to rise up against the Protectors—"

"We'd have an actual shot of getting out," Octavia cut in, her eyes ablaze, her face flushed with hope.

"Spread the word to the girls you trust. Tell them to get ready to run, but make sure they don't act suspicious. I'm going to do the same with the guys. We don't want the Protectors to have their guard up during the Pairing Ceremony, we want them to think we're all going along with it happily." He paused, thinking. "Get word to Glass too, if you can. What's the latest with the boats? Will we know what to do when we get to them?"

"Oh, I think we'll be fine. I've been practicing rowing."

Wells's jaw dropped. "What? *When?*"

"I convinced the Protector that oversees my laundry shift that we also needed to be cleaning the boats, since they were touching the precious river. She's had me on boat-cleaning duty ever since, and whenever the Protectors look away, I grab a paddle and have at it."

He shook his head with a smile. "You're amazing, O."

She shrugged and grinned. "I have my moments." Then she grabbed the tray up and walked quickly out of the room.

After Wells finished eating, Oak came back to escort him to his quarters. As they walked, the older man droned on incessantly. "Mother says we're going to put roots here," he said. "But that doesn't mean our work stops. We're going to go up and down the coast. There may be other settlements in the area, and we'll find them. We're going to set up more fortresses like this one until there's no one left but us, if Earth wills it."

"If Earth wills it." Wells's tone was dripping with sarcasm, but Oak didn't notice.

The Protector clasped Wells's shoulder as they rounded the corner. "You're going to be a part of that, boy. You've proven yourself now. You'll be real useful, I can tell."

"I appreciate that, Oak," Wells said darkly.

When they reached the barracks, Wells saw the two Protectors who had dragged him into the basement only hours earlier to be interrogated. They grinned at him now, clapping him on the arm.

"We heard you made your first sacrifice tonight," one said, eyebrows raised. "Earth be good. Welcome to the fold."

Wells forced a "thank you" past clenched lips. Was that what these people called the murders they committed? A *sacrifice*?

Oak held the door to the sleeping quarters open for Wells, then led him to his cage. All of the other guys were already in their cages, asleep.

"Get some rest, son," Oak said, locking him in. "At sunrise tomorrow, you officially become a Protector—and you're going to want all of your energy for that. We'll be back to get you soon."

When Oak had left the room, Wells curled up on the mat in his cage. "Eric," he whispered to the cot next to him.

Eric didn't respond. From the steady pattern of his heavy breaths, it was clear he was fast asleep.

A pit formed in Wells's stomach. If he couldn't talk to the guys tonight, he'd have to try to get to them all in the morning. He hoped it'd be enough.

———

The door to their sleeping quarters slammed open. "Rise and shine, recruits," Oak shouted cheerily. He walked up and down the row of cages, unlocking them all. "It's almost sunrise. Get dressed, and we'll be back to collect you soon. You'll become Protectors today, if Earth wills it."

As Oak strolled back out of the room, all of the guys crawled out of their cages. Wells tried to make eye contact with Eric and Kit, but they both looked quickly away.

The young recruit who'd been with him at the farm site glanced over at Wells. "We heard you killed Graham."

So this was why their eyes were all shuttered. They weren't sure if they could trust him.

"I didn't," Wells answered bluntly. "Graham killed himself to save the rest of us."

He held his breath as a ripple of murmurs passed through the crowded room.

Wells strode forward. "All Graham wanted was to get home to his people, but he died a *hero* instead."

His shoulders taut as bowstrings, Wells watched the dozen or so recruits that were not from their camp, checking each of their reactions. They were exchanging nervous glances, but underneath that knee-jerk response, Wells could see vulnerability.

He could see them starting to hope.

He walked up to the young recruit from the farm. "What's your name?" Wells asked.

"Cob," the boy said, eyes wide with apprehension.

"Cob," Wells repeated, smiling. "It's good to meet you. I'm Wells. Where are you from, Cob?"

The room drew in a scattered gasp at the question. Wells knew the question was taboo; they were supposed to have washed away their pasts in the river.

"I'm from . . . from *here*," Cob sputtered. "I'm from the Stone."

Wells shook his head, patient. "Before that."

Cob paled, but he drew a deep breath. "I'm . . . from the mountains."

"Tell me about it."

"It's a small . . ." His head sank. "*Was* a small village in a mountain valley, a week's journey from here. The Protectors found us and recruited me as they made their way to the Stone. We kept sheep and goats. My mom worked the wool and my pa . . . my pa . . ." His voice dwindled, choked by the memories of all he'd lost. He shook his head, his eyes filling up.

Wells pressed a hand to his shoulder, then moved down the row to a heavyset recruit a little older than the others. "How about you?"

"We washed all that away in the river," the recruit said brusquely, his expression closed off.

Wells nodded, considering. Either this guy was a true believer or he thought this was a test. There was so much fear rippling through the room, Wells could practically feel it. The older recruit was watching him with suspicion.

"*My* home," Wells said, his voice rising, "is a few days west of here. It's a camp that a hundred of us built with our hands and our sweat and our blood after crash-landing on the planet. We fought hard to make a home there . . . and I will be *damned* if I'm going to wash the memory of it away, just because a bunch of murderers told me '*Earth wills it.*'" He raised his hands to make air quotes, rewarded by the sound of a few tentative laughs.

"I wake up every morning thinking that I'm there," Wells went on, his heart pounding. "And when I remember what happened to the place I love, the people I love, the only thing that gets me out of that"—he pointed to his empty cage—"is *revenge*."

Several of the men were nodding now. Eric glanced at Kit, their eyes shining with quiet hope.

"Your minds are your own," Wells said, his voice rising as he paced up and down the row. "But I'm going to tell you what I think. I think that river washed *nothing* away. I think you're still there, all of you, strong and angry as ever." He pointed to the closed door. "I don't know if they're human anymore. But *we* are. Our memories matter. Our homes matter. Our people matter."

The men stood up now, one after another, their faces bright as torches, burning with rage.

"I think I'm not going to live another second as one of them," Wells shouted, the others roaring back in agreement. "When they take us to the Heart of the Stone, we will fight back. Our captivity ends today. *Who's*—?"

A colossal, deafening bang echoed through the walls, the floor, into his very bones. Wells careened to the side. Plaster fell from the ceiling. The rest of the rebels rose slowly from where they'd fallen, getting their balance as they looked frantically around.

"What's happening?" Eric shouted.

Someone's blowing down the freaking walls, Wells thought, but before he could voice that theory, there came another boom, this one closer. It felt as if the walls around them were going to crumble. Wells struggled upward and staggered to the door.

"Let's move!" he shouted to the others, waiting to wave them through the doorway.

"Where are we going?" asked Cob, grabbing Wells's arm as he passed.

Another explosion rocked the floor, the sound of screams joining with the clattering din, so loud that Wells had to shout to be heard.

"How does home sound?" he yelled.

Cob shot him a wild grin. "It sounds just about perfect!"

CHAPTER *28*

Glass

It was the darkest hour before the sunrise, and it was about to happen.

The Pairing Ceremony.

Margot had shaken Glass awake a few minutes ago, and instructed her to go get the other female recruits. To lead them to their fates. Glass's knees trembled as she got out of her bed and pulled on her white dress, braiding her hair back.

This wasn't supposed to be happening. Wells was supposed to have figured out an escape plan by now. Was it possible that Octavia hadn't been able to find him? Or maybe her friends left without her. Her stomach felt leaden, filled with dread.

Half in a daze, Glass moved throughout the dark corridors of the Stone, Margot trailing behind her. When they reached the women's den, Margot unlocked the door. Glass stepped in, hands shaking.

All the girls were awake already, sitting on their mats, tidily made up for the Ceremony. Glass caught Octavia's eye, but Octavia kept her face schooled, giving away nothing.

"It's time," Glass told them. The girls filed past her and out the door, Octavia quickly squeezing her hand.

Margot led the front of the line, Glass following in the back. She kept her step steady, but her eyes darted everywhere—the crumbling alley to the left, the jagged path past a heap of rubble to the right, searching frantically for a way out of here, away from this.

It wasn't too late. Instead of continuing to walk to the Heart of the Stone, she could grab her friends and lead them in the opposite direction. She could keep them going until they reached the outer gates. But then what?

Could they possibly fight their way past the Protectors posted at every exit? And even if they did make it out, was she strong enough to make sure they could all escape and survive out there, with winter looming and god knew what other dangers lying in wait?

Glass stopped walking, closing her eyes. She drew a

determined breath, ready to warn the white-clad young women about what lay ahead. But before she could speak a single word, Octavia darted back to her and gripped her arm, her eyes flashing a warning. Far ahead at the front of the line, Margot was oblivious.

"Not yet," Octavia hissed into Glass's ear. "Wells has a plan. It's happening soon. We just need to be ready to run."

Octavia slunk forward to take her place in the tidy line. Stunned, Glass scanned the rest of them and saw a grim line to their mouths, a fearful but steely glint in their eyes. They all knew.

Glass blinked at Octavia. Octavia nodded once, then lifted her chin and stared blankly ahead.

Onward, then.

Glass kept them moving, her own heart flailing in her chest, all the way to the Heart of the Stone.

It wasn't until they walked in that her step faltered. This couldn't be it. She must have made a wrong turn. Glass knew every inch of this place by now, mapped in her mind as if etched there permanently, so she was sure she'd taken them to the right place. But no . . . this was impossible.

In the center of the orchard was a grotesque construction: a carefully erected gazebo made of bones—*human* bones. And on it stood the High Protector, looking beatific, like a priestess waiting to bless her flock.

Peering down at the line of girls, Soren's eyes landed on Glass and she gave her that loving smile, the one that had previously made Glass feel warm, like she belonged, like she was special. But now Glass saw the truth behind that smile: Her sweet, maternal nature hid the fact that she was brainwashing all her people. Convincing them with her gentleness that something as awful as this Pairing Ceremony was good and natural.

Glass turned, searching desperately for Wells, as Soren began to speak. So far, only the female recruits had been brought into the Heart of the Stone.

"My children. Welcome. Today, I stand upon bones that were once buried in the Earth, bones of the selfish takers whose greed brought on the Cataclysm. As Protectors, it is our duty to take pollutants like this out of our beloved Earth. The Pairing Ceremony is our promise to Earth, so we perform it standing on these bones as a reminder that we have formed a better, more thoughtful society. As Earth has brought you to us, now we must give back to Earth, planting seeds that will . . ."

Glass could hardly hear her through the pounding of her own heart. She glanced right to see Octavia perched on the balls of her feet, ready to run.

Glass closed her eyes, picturing the best way out of

here. West and then south and then straight through the narrow, jagged alley and out to the fields . . . she just needed to wait for the—

A great, shattering boom drowned out Glass's thoughts and Soren's speech.

By the time Glass opened her eyes again, the ground was lurching beneath her feet. She knew only too well what this was. An explosion . . . the kind that destroyed everything in its path. Just like the explosions that had rocked her camp.

But this time, judging by the looks on the Protectors' faces, they weren't the ones dropping the bombs.

A second explosion went off; both had come from around the outer walls of the Stone. Based on the way the ground was shaking, though, the entire structural integrity of the compound was being compromised. And the ground wasn't the only thing shaking—the gazebo started to sway, bones tumbling out of it.

"Get back!" Glass shouted, pushing the girls toward the exit of the courtyard.

Soren looked stunned for a moment; then her head whipped around to her advisors. "Find the men and get to the armory!"

Without a blink, the women in gray turned on

their heels and sprinted out of the courtyard as she'd commanded.

Soren started making her way out of the gazebo, but as she came toward them, the gazebo's bone floor shifted and one of her legs fell through it. She peered up and reached toward Glass. "Help me out . . . quickly!"

Glass turned to the other girls and spoke in a rush. "Run west, toward the water. Take the alleys, those walls are thicker, less likely to fall."

"Glass!" Soren called.

"Go," Glass said to the others, ignoring the confused question in Octavia's and Anna's eyes . . . why wasn't she coming too? Then she turned back to Soren, whose hand was extended, asking for help, just as another blast seemed to tilt the very planet off its axis.

This one was too much for the gazebo to withstand. The entire behemoth leaned forward, back, and forward again, careening downward, crushing everything in its path.

Including Soren.

A cloud of dust shot out from every direction. Glass hacked a cough, covering her eyes, as she heard the girls behind her racing away, shouting directions to one another. She staggered forward, squinting to see through the gritty air.

As the dust drifted away, Glass saw a figure still there, eyes open, hand stretched out to reach hers.

The High Protector was trapped under what was left of the gazebo, now no more than a pile of bones.

"Get me out," Soren said, her voice no longer remotely calm. "Glass, you have to help me."

Glass crept closer, her eyes wandering to the nearest wall. A massive metal support beam had been knocked loose in the aftershock of the last explosion. It wavered away from the wall dangerously. All it would take was a gust of wind and it would come crashing down on both of them.

"Don't look at that, look at me," Soren said, straining so hard for her old, sweet, soothing tone that the sound of it made Glass stagger backward, repelled. The older woman smiled, her eyes like daggers.

Glass glanced over at the huge metal beam, wavering wildly. For one split second, she pictured herself diving forward, digging Soren out, pushing her out of the way as the beam fell. Then she pictured something else. The image of Glass's mother leaping in front of her, begging for Glass's life to be spared. Dying to make that wish come true.

"My child, I'm begging you," Soren said.

"I'm not your child," Glass said, shaking her head in disgust. "None of us are."

Soren's mouth drew in, all warmth evaporating like a mirage in the desert sun.

Glass retreated a few feet more. "You've never had a mother, have you? A real one?"

Soren closed her eyes, not responding.

Another step. "Well, *I* had a mother once. Do you know what they do, out there in the real world? They protect their children." Glass felt all emotion draining out of her, remembering her camp, her village, the wagon that dragged her away, room after room of this hellhole filled with grieving prisoners, and *all* of this repeated again and again, inflicted on generation after generation. "You do the opposite, Soren. You manipulate your people to kill anything in your way. You do the opposite of protecting your children—you offer them up in this horrible ceremony. You're not a mother." She shrugged. "Just a parasite."

As another blast shook the eastern walls, the ground shook under Glass's feet.

"I'll die if you leave me here!" Soren called out, her voice fading to nothing.

Glass bit back a swell of tears, fighting the urge to turn back.

"Only if Earth wills it," she said.

West through the alleys, Glass thought, starting away.

Out to the fields and then keep running, keep running, keep running.

A great shrieking whine sounded from behind her. That beam was finally giving way.

Glass heard Soren screaming.

Her heart broke, despite it all. But she kept on running.

CHAPTER *29*

Clarke

Clarke held her breath, watching the last grenade explode along the massive outer wall, brilliant orange searing her eyes. The sound of it made her flinch, just as the last three detonations had.

Beside her, Bellamy let out an exultant huff, while Luke rocked back onto his heels, grinning in relief. Four explosives. Four successful detonations. Now all that was left to do was invade.

Clarke poked her head above the rubble, watching the silhouettes of Felix, Jessa, and Vale hurry into the gaping hole their bombs had carved into the outer wall of the compound. Paul had stayed behind at their campsite like the coward that he was.

Luke started to rise, but Bellamy held his hand up. "Wait for Felix's signal that the coast is clear."

Clarke gripped the crumbling cinder blocks in front of her, staring unblinking at the spot the others had just disappeared into. She drew in an anxious breath, hearing the rat-a-tat of new gunfire rising above the groaning of the building and roar of the flames.

Please let it be us doing the firing, she prayed, her fingers tightening reluctantly around her own handgun in preparation.

Felix appeared in the distance, waving a lit torch above his head. He glanced behind him, and then quickly ducked back inside.

Bellamy hissed, "There. Let's move."

They sprinted across the heap of rubble where they'd taken cover. Clarke ran until her lungs burned, covering her face with her arm as they approached the plumes of smoke from the explosions. She tried not to look up at the building, somehow even more terrifying a behemoth now that it was visibly crumbling. They'd need to get in and out fast or they were going to be destroyed right along with the rest of it.

She cocked her gun and strode inside, blood pumping hard, eyes darting in every direction. Bellamy took the lead, while Luke provided cover from the side, all of them stunned by the sight of the place. It was like a bombed-out walled city. Clarke wasn't sure how much damage was from their grenades and how much had happened long ago. But Luke's plan to undermine the foundations of the walls was working better than anyone could have dreamed. Too well, in fact.

The walls were buckling, huge chunks falling from above, the whole thing letting out a deep metallic groan.

"You guys go find the others, before this whole thing collapses!" Clarke said, pointing in the opposite direction. "I'll find Felix, Jessa, and Vale and head to the armory with them."

Luke started off quickly, undoubtedly thinking of Glass's presence somewhere in the building, but Bellamy hesitated for a pained moment before turning to join him.

Clarke braced herself and turned, weapon raised, just as a white-clad mob rounded the corner of the debris-strewn road and raced toward her. Clarke raised her gun, setting its sights on the tallest of them. But then one of the raiders turned . . . and Clarke nearly dropped her weapon in shock.

It was Wells.

He looked just as stunned by the sight of her, but he recovered fast and covered the space between them in five quick strides, pulling her in for a quick hug.

"You're all right!" she said, stepping away for a relieved look at him.

"I am," he replied, wiping sweat off his brow.

"Eric?" she asked.

He pointed behind him at the tall one she'd nearly shot. "He's fine."

"Graham?"

Wells shook his head, pain sparking in his eyes.

Clarke peered over his shoulder at the group of raiders behind him. "Are they . . . ?"

"They're with us," Wells said. "Or they want to be. I can explain everything."

A rumble sounded from above. Clarke peered up to see a thick crack creeping down the wall face. She grabbed Wells's elbow and yanked him away from it.

"Explain outside," Clarke shouted over the din. "We need to get out of here before the whole thing collapses."

They raced outside through the hole their grenades had made. As they put distance between themselves and the crumbling walls, Wells filled Clarke in on how he'd rallied the other recruits—they'd been prepared to riot at some sort of mass gathering this morning, but then the first grenade went off and all hell broke loose.

"What was the plan?" he asked her as they turned and watched the entrance to the Stone collapse. "You guys were going to blow down the structure with us inside?"

Clarke winced. "No, it was just supposed to knock down the outer walls. We just wanted to get in so we could rescue you all. But we didn't anticipate how much damage there had already been to the foundations."

Wells stared back at the building, his face grim. "We knocked out the people guarding us and managed to escape, but the girls are still in there. I think the rest of the Protectors headed to their armory. They're not going to give this place up easily, Clarke. We need to be prepared for a fight."

Clarke grinned. "Oh, we are. If they're headed to the armory, they're in for a nasty surprise."

She jogged to the perimeter of the forest, Wells following behind her. There, hidden under the brush, were all the weapons they'd stolen.

Wells's eyes widened; then he shouted for all the other guys to come over. One by one, they each grabbed a gun and armed themselves. If the Protectors wanted a fight, they'd be ready for them.

Wells looked back at the fortress, his eyes determined.

"We need to help the girls get out of there. Let's go around to the west side of the building—there's an entrance there. If it's still guarded, we can fight our way in."

Clarke bit back a smile. The Wells she knew—the confident leader—was finally back. "Lead the way."

———

They approached the building from the western side, and all was eerily quiet. The guards had abandoned this entrance. Wells shot Clarke a warning look and darted ahead to make sure the coast was clear. Then he waved her and the other men into the building.

"Which way?" she asked him, peering around the dark halls. There hadn't been any damage to this side of the building yet, but in the distance, Clarke heard the walls continuing to fall. They wouldn't have long.

"The girls were probably in the Heart of the Stone, so . . ." Wells glanced around, then nodded to their left. "This way."

But before they could get much deeper into the building, they heard the rumbling of a crowd of people headed toward them. Clarke and the guys steadied their weapons, waiting for the raiders.

To her surprise, the approaching mob was made up of girls, all of them dressed in white dresses down to their ankles, their hair flying loose around their shoulders.

"Clarke!" one of them screamed.

Clarke blinked, dizzy, and let the front line start to pass her. *Octavia?*

And there she was, eyes bright as ever. A grateful sob rose in Clarke's throat. She opened her arms wide and Octavia bounded into them, wrapping her in a frantic hug. These girls hadn't needed saving—they'd already been saving themselves.

"Was that you guys?" Octavia asked, cocking her head east. She moved to give Wells a quick hug.

Clarke nodded.

A curly-haired girl standing beside Octavia glanced upward in awe, grinning. "Badass."

"Clarke, Anna, Anna, Clarke . . ." Octavia waved her hand in the air. "How about we skip the rest of the introductions until after we escape?"

"Good plan," Clarke said, starting to run beside them. "Where's Glass?"

"I don't know," Octavia said, her breath growing ragged as they ran. "But she knows the plan. We'll find her."

Wells led them all back toward the exit, but before they could get there, Clarke felt herself yanked violently backward. Her pulse spiked straight into sharp terror.

She was yanked down to the ground. A blond woman in a gray dress stood above her, her eyes full of inhuman rage. The woman was holding a dagger high . . . and aiming it straight for Clarke's neck.

A fist connected with the attacker's face. The woman let go with a gasp, her head knocking against the rocky wall, the rest of her slumping to the ground with it. Clarke looked up to see Octavia wincing, cradling her own bloodied hand.

Anna beamed. "She's been waiting to do that *forever.*"

"Is that woman one of their leaders?" Clarke asked, staggering upright. "Maybe we should take her—use her to negotiate—"

"A truce?" Wells supplied darkly.

"Why not?" Clarke swiped dirt off her cheek. "They have no weapons left. We hold all the leverage," Clarke said, her eyes still locked on Wells.

"Fine," Wells said. "Let's take her."

They'd made it ten more steps toward the exit when a sound made them stop in their tracks . . . a guttural, animalistic cry made by *way* too many voices.

Two stunned seconds later, a group of familiar figures—Bellamy, Luke, Felix, Jessa, and Vale—erupted around the corner. Their friends raced toward them, arms and legs pumping wildly. Bellamy's eyes widened at the sight of Clarke, and then flooded with relief when they landed on Octavia, but then they narrowed as he screamed a single word.

"Run!"

Clarke turned and fled with the crowd. Outside, the sun was rising, fiery, on the horizon. And behind them, the building mirrored the colors, engulfed in actual flames. Their crowd of escapees kept sprinting until they spotted a rippling movement in the near distance. Water. They'd reached the river.

Backing up until she stood shoulder to shoulder with Bellamy, Clarke turned and recocked her gun, preparing for a last stand. A crowd of raiders came roaring out of the building. This was it.

There was no mistaking it this time—these people were their enemies. Clarke stood on the front line as a crowd of men in white, some armed with guns, others with sticks and rocks, charged forward at full speed. They were led by a trio of women in gray dresses. Which reminded Clarke...

She grabbed the gray woman who had attacked her in the hall and stepped forward, pressing her gun to the woman's head.

"Stop," Clarke shouted at the approaching raiders. "Or I shoot her."

The raiders halted, the women in front looking wild-eyed.

"We have your weapons," continued Clarke. "We have your captives. *Our* people. Your building is destroyed. You are outnumbered and you cannot win. But this doesn't need to end in violence. Leave. Leave this area and leave us be, and never, ever come back."

All the people behind her watched silently as their pursuers lowered their weapons and dropped their rocks, their faces falling slack. They looked . . . *defeated*.

But then one of the women in gray stepped forward, her eyes blazing. "No. Soren declared this our home. She said that Earth willed it. We won't leave unless Soren says so."

Before Clarke could reply, Anna said, "Oh god," and pointed past her shoulder.

A lone figure in white was crawling through a blown-out window behind them, flames licking at her back.

"Is that Glass?" Clarke asked, squinting.

Everyone—raiders and rescuers and captives alike—turned to watch her approach. Glass stumbled closer, dirty and defiant.

"Soren . . . is dead," Glass shouted.

CHAPTER *30*

Glass

Still reeling from Soren's last haunting scream, Glass shivered as she walked toward her friends.

All along the edge of the crumbling building, the Protectors were backing up, laying down their rocks and sticks, even their guns, with a confused glaze to their eyes. The warriors looked suddenly completely lost, helpless to do anything.

Without Soren, they were nothing.

And Glass and her friends were safe. They were free.

A hot gust of wind blew suddenly from the direction of the Stone. Glass pictured the flames devouring everything and everyone in their path, starting with the space that used to be an orchard . . . Then she sucked in a breath and forced her eyes away, turning instead to gaze out at the eastern side of the river. Dawn was breaking, the broad orange sun bright enough to extinguish all images of the burning fortress from Glass's mind.

She blinked a few times while her eyes adjusted, turning a murky silhouette into a tall young man . . . someone impossibly, heartbreakingly familiar.

Glass's mouth fell open.

He smiled and a sob lodged itself in Glass's throat. She touched her own face first to make sure this was happening in real life . . . that she was actually alive and conscious and actually, truly seeing him standing in front of her . . . Then she reached out and touched his cheeks with the tips of her fingers, carefully, as though he might break.

He wasn't a hallucination. He was solid, his pulse thrumming steadily, his breath a little shaky as she ran her hands along his lips, his neck, his chest.

Then and only then did she dare say it: "*Luke*."

Her eyes teared up at the sound of the name and even more at the sight of his answering grin. She slid her arms around his neck and kissed him, and as their kiss deepened, all fear dropped away, replaced by wonder and burning, all-consuming gratitude.

"You're cold," he said, just as she was thinking how warm he was. He pulled away, brow knitted. "Are you going to be okay?"

Glass let out a dazed laugh. "Everything is perfect."

"Okay, folks," a confident male voice shouted. It was Paul, one of the guards from their camp. "It looks like the fire might spread, so we should walk alongside the river to be safe."

Luke scoffed and shook his head, exchanging bemused glances with Bellamy. "That guy is unbelievable."

Clarke let out a short laugh. "Unfortunately he's right, though. Shall we?"

They made a quiet procession, considering how many of them there were, but the air around the entire group was charged with relief and hope.

Luke glanced around, eyes wide. "Where did all these people *come* from?"

"All over," Glass said, her glance landing back on Anna and Octavia, walking along with a number of other girls from the dormitories. "Some were taken from their homes, like we were, and dragged here. Some are Colonists from a dropship that went off course and crashed."

"What?" Luke's head whipped around. "Anyone you know?" She knew he was thinking of all the friends he left behind on Walden to accompany Glass to Earth.

"No, but I haven't had a chance to meet everyone yet."

He swiveled his head from side to side, then let out a quiet sigh when he didn't spot anyone he recognized.

They walked in silence around the curve of the river bend. As they went, they saw one last Protector stare after them with empty eyes.

Ahead of her, Wells shuddered to a stop.

"Do you know him?" Glass asked.

Wells nodded. "He was my trainer. Oak."

After a long moment, Oak turned and limped back toward the Stone.

"They'll regroup," Luke said, his voice tight. "We should expect a skirmish as soon as we start back west—"

"I doubt it," Glass cut in quietly. "They don't have anyone commanding them anymore. It'll take them longer than a few hours to figure out how to start thinking for themselves. They'll have to find their way back to other groups of Protectors, and there aren't any other settlements near here, at least not from what I'd gathered. I don't think we'll have to worry about them again." She paused, thinking about everything they'd just experienced. "The explosions. Were those you?"

Luke grinned. Then his brow furrowed. "It wasn't my neatest work. We only had an hour to plant the explosives and I never got a clear look at the foundations . . ."

"You saved all these people, Luke," Glass said, squeezing his arm.

"I'm glad. But honestly . . . ?" He pulled her closer. "There was only one person I was thinking about saving. I didn't expect it to do that much damage, Glass. If you hadn't come out of there all right . . . I don't know what I would have done."

"Don't think about that," Glass said quickly, pushing a curly lock of hair out of his eyes. "You did what you had to do. Now just . . . look forward."

Luke's gaze was distant as his mind worked. Glass's heart swelled at the familiar look. It felt so good to be back by his side.

"Let's head toward the woods at the next bend in the river and set up a camp with a well-guarded perimeter. Light a fire, get these people warm."

Glass smiled in approval, but Luke was still thinking.

"And then we can head west, back to our camp tomorrow." He shook his head, his eyes landing on hers. "But what about the rest of them?"

"They'll go back to their own homes, I guess. Or make new ones." She took his hand and lifted it to her lips. "You've given them that chance."

Luke motioned to Wells, up ahead, and Wells nodded briskly, veering west.

As they reached the bend, Glass realized she didn't have a clear picture of what they were even going home to. Had it been destroyed completely or had her people fought back? Either way, there would be some rebuilding ahead. And she would do what she could to help. She'd make this world her home.

Glass stood on the riverbank and peered up at the morning sky, searching in vain for a tiny speck of light, the place where they used to live.

Thank you, she silently called out, her eyes blurring and spilling over. *I made it, Mom. I'm still here. I still exist. And I'll never stop saying thank you.*

CHAPTER *31*

Bellamy

They needed to chop wood for the bonfire and hunt dinner to feed their friends and their new allies, but as far as Bellamy was concerned, all that could wait—because his little sister was telling him about her girlfriend.

"She's from Walden, maybe you knew her. I didn't, but it seems like we've known each other, like, forever . . ." Octavia blushed to almost the color of her hair ribbon. "She's just ridiculously funny. I mean, even with everything that was going on, she could always find something to make me laugh . . ."

Bellamy couldn't stop grinning, and it wasn't just because of Octavia's enthusiasm. It was the simple fact that she was here, standing in front of him, safe and sound and acting like the only thing that happened this past week was meeting Anna.

Everything that Octavia had faced over her lifetime would have broken a weaker person. But Bellamy's sister was as resilient as steel. As ever, his pride for her verged on awe. He shook his head slightly, listening to her go on.

"And she's got a serious knack for invention! Her brain is incredible, I'm telling you. She was training to work on the plumbing systems back on the ship, but she's helping Luke make torches right now and I was thinking if those two get to talking, back at camp, she could make a real contribution to . . . *What?*"

Octavia put her hands on her hips. She'd finally noticed Bellamy's amused expression—but was reading it completely wrong.

Bellamy laughed, arms wide. "I'm sold! Your girlfriend is clearly brilliant and wonderful and you are even more clearly crazy about her."

Octavia bit her lip, looking at her feet. "I don't know if she's my *girlfriend* exactly."

Bellamy raised an eyebrow. "Still want to play the field?"

Her smile crept upward. "No, I just haven't asked her."

"So ask her now," he said, nudging her shoulder.

"Seriously, go do it. Right this second. Nothing's guaranteed down here, O. We have to seize the chances we've got."

She drew a giddy breath. "I really think you're going to like her."

Bellamy had never seen Octavia look more nervous. He pulled her into a hug and said, "Of *course* I'll like her."

Octavia peered up at him, eyes glittering; then she darted off across the small sandy inlet to find Anna. As Bellamy watched her go, his eyes drifted over the makeshift campsite and landed on Clarke.

She was kneeling beside the bonfire, tending to one of the escapees who'd been injured by falling debris. She looked so determined, so capable, so caring, that Bellamy's breath caught in his chest.

And right then, he knew beyond certainty that the only future worth living was one with her in it.

Wells came in from the forest, hauling branches for the fire. Bellamy shook himself out of his reverie and strode over to him. "Could you use any help?"

Wells wiped his forehead, heaving a breath. "I think we're good on wood for now, but we'll need to prepare one of Bellamy's kills for dinner. Or . . . all of his kills," he said, glancing around at the crowd.

Bellamy shrugged, smiling. "Don't worry. We'll figure it out as we go."

"It's worked out so far, hasn't it?" Wells said, attempting an exhausted smile.

"Hell, yeah," Bellamy said, clapping a hand on his brother's shoulder. "You managed to rally all those recruits and saved . . . how many people? Forty?"

"Fifty-four," Wells said quietly. He scratched his cheek. "I took a quick tally."

Bellamy nodded. "That's a whole lot of people who got out, thanks to you."

"Thanks to both of us," Wells said, patting Bellamy on the back. His face turned grave, and pain flickered in his eyes.

"What happened?" Bellamy asked. "What's wrong?"

"Graham didn't make it," Wells said.

"They . . . they killed him?" Bellamy said hoarsely. There'd been a point where he'd wanted to kill Graham himself, but that felt like a lifetime ago. Graham had worked hard to become a helpful member of their new community, and the thought of his lifeless body somewhere still in that godforsaken fortress sent a surprisingly sharp stab of pain through his chest.

Wells took a deep breath. "He . . . he sacrificed himself to save the rest of us. He died doing something far more heroic and brave than anything I could've done."

They both fell silent for a long moment as they turned

and looked over the scattered crowd. Some were clustered around the fire, soaking up the heat. Others were hard at work preparing for the road and the journey ahead of them. A few milled around the forest, looking shocked that they were able to walk around freely.

"I wonder where they're all going to go," Wells said.

Bellamy shrugged. "My guess would be . . . wherever *you* go."

Wells's eyes clouded, more thoughtful than worried. "That would be all right, wouldn't it? If they came back with us?"

"The more the merrier, as far as I'm concerned," Bellamy said. "But I think it's your call to make."

Wells shook his head. "You're the Councilor, not me. You should be the one to decide."

It'd mean more mouths to feed, bodies to shelter. But what the hell? This planet was big enough for all of them. He'd just have to make sure some of them actually knew how to hunt.

Clarke was standing by the fire now, dusting off her hands. He strode over to her.

"How are they doing?" he asked Clarke, gesturing to the patients.

"Okay, I think. Anxious to get going. I think we'll all feel better once we've put more distance between us and . . ." She nodded nervously to the southeast.

Bellamy's shoulders tensed. Following the river had already taken them several miles away from the Protectors' fortress, but he agreed. The sooner they could get back to their own camp, the better.

"We have torches!" Octavia shouted, running in from the forest with the famous Anna trailing behind her, grinning, their arms full of mossy branches wrapped in wet cloth.

"Okay, so I *do* realize it's still light out," Anna said drily, blinking up at the cloudy morning sky. "But I thought these would be helpful once we make camp for the night, since not everyone is going to be able to sleep around that." She motioned to the bonfire, sending nearly all the torches tumbling out of her arms. Bellamy stooped to help her gather them back up. "Gah! Coordination. Not my strong suit."

Bellamy laughed. He liked her already.

Octavia went very red and then blurted, "So, Bellamy. I'd like you to meet my *girlfriend*, Anna."

Bellamy grinned and shook her hand. "Nice to meet you, Anna. I'm glad you're coming with us."

Octavia took Anna's hand and intertwined their fingers. "I can't wait to bring you home."

The word *home* resounded like a chime in Bellamy's chest. Despite the journey ahead of them, he somehow felt as though he was already there. Home was wherever your family was. And for the first time in a week, they were all back together. His sister was safe and happy. His brother was alive and acting more like himself than he had in a month. And Clarke . . .

Bellamy smiled slowly over at her, realizing he'd included her as a family member.

Then his heart started to beat, louder and louder, more and more certain.

This is what family means. The people you fight for. The people you can't live without. Bellamy peered out over the road ahead with dawning exhilaration.

There's something I have to do.

CHAPTER *32*

Wells

They were feverish, they were muddy, they were exhausted . . . but there it was: the split tree that marked the path into camp.

After two days' hard travel from the Stone, they were home.

However they did this, he wanted to make it quick. Everyone needed a fire and a meal and a good rest. Wells hoped that they'd be able to find those things here, that they weren't about to walk into even more chaos and destruction.

Behind him, Kit and Jessa and the other Earthborns let out a happy shout, realizing where they were. Wells grinned too, but quickly raised a hand.

"We should wait here, send an advance party," Wells called out. "Our camp will be on edge after everything that's happened, and not everybody here is a familiar face."

His eyes drifted over the crowd; more than half of them were total strangers to the people in their camp. Along the way, some of the escapees had veered off to go in search of their own homes, wanting to reclaim the places that had been stolen from them. Others had wanted to start fresh, and had joined their journey here.

But regardless of where they'd gone, all of the escapees were fueled by defiance and bright hope. From the ashes of the Stone, a new community had emerged, reshaped in a way the Protectors never could have imagined.

Wells drew a breath, thinking. Then he pointed to people in the crowd: an Earthborn, a rescue party member, and a new face.

"Kit, Clarke . . . and Cob. Come with me."

Kit and Clarke both strode forward purposefully, but Cob glanced around as if confused.

Wells smiled encouragingly, waving him over. "Once they meet you, they won't be worried about strangers anymore."

The younger boy grinned and hurried to join them, while the others settled in to wait behind.

Then, united as one, the four of them strode toward the camp.

A crashing sound echoed in the near distance and Cob let out a yelp. Wells glanced over at him and realized that Cob's ankle was wrapped around a trip wire. It must have caused that noise, sounded some sort of alarm.

"It's okay," Wells said to the boy as a line of Colonist guards crashed through the bushes, shouting for them to get on their knees.

They all raised their hands and obeyed, falling into the wet dirt just as one of the guards yelled, "Clarke! Wells! I can't believe it . . . you made it! You freaking *made* it!"

Clarke peered up with a smile, exhaling slowly. "Willa. It's so good to see you!"

Willa offered Clarke a hand up, and the other six lowered their guns, glancing around at one another with their eyes igniting.

"Just the four of you?" one of them asked.

"We've left a slightly bigger crowd a half mile back," Wells said. "It's all of our captives, our rescuers . . . and then some."

The guards exchanged a wary look.

"Take us to the Council," Wells ordered. "They can decide what we'll do next . . . if we'll welcome in these new friends."

Willa shot him an appraising look, and shrugged. "That sounds fine to me." She turned to lead the way. The other guards glanced at one another, then followed after her.

"You've got this," Kit whispered as they started into camp. Wells glanced at him, surprised. Kit smiled. "If you could convince a bunch of terrified cult members to start a rebellion, I *think* you can talk our people into taking in a few refugees."

"I hope you're right," Wells said, bracing himself as they came upon the first sight of the camp.

It wasn't pretty, but there were also signs of hope. A deer was roasting over a cooking fire on one side of the camp, while men and women were hard at work rebuilding log cabins on the other. The infirmary was still intact, a comforting line of smoke rising upward from its chimney.

Clarke's step quickened at the sight of it. He knew she couldn't wait to get to her parents.

"Go ahead," he told her. She grinned and sprinted toward it, her long hair flying behind her.

Kit veered off too, rushing to greet some Earthborn friends who were teaching a group of Colonists how to grind grain for bread.

That left Wells and Cob and the guards headed to the camp's central bonfire, where two men stood in stooped conversation.

Rhodes was the first to turn, then Max. The Earthborn leader's face went from shocked to joyous in a single blink. Before Wells could get a word out, Max crossed the space between them with his arms wide open, gathering Wells in a tight hug, a sob bursting out of his throat.

"My boy," he said, bringing tears to Wells's eyes. "You made it. I hoped, but I didn't know . . ." He drew back, beaming. Then he nodded, proudly. "You made it home."

"Not all of us made it," Wells said, swallowing down a lump in his throat. "We . . . we lost Graham." He winced, imagining the look on Lila's face when he told her. Although she played it cool, Wells knew she'd started to develop real feelings for Graham over the past few weeks.

"I brought others too," Wells said. "Some are Colonists, believe it or not, from a dropship that landed to the south of here. And some"—he motioned to Cob—"are new friends altogether."

Behind Max, Rhodes raised his eyebrows, disbelief apparent on his face. "New . . . ? How many?"

"Fifty-four at last count, though a few people left in search of their former homes. And I'll vouch for our new friends myself . . . they're good people."

Max and Rhodes exchanged a look. Then Rhodes nodded.

"If you trust them, we trust them," Rhodes said. "And

we could certainly use all the help we can get in rebuilding for the winter. Bring them in. Were you followed?" he asked, glancing at the guards. "Do we need to establish a perimeter?"

"No more than you're doing. I think," Wells said. "Between our uprising and everything your search party managed to do, I don't think we'll need to worry about the Protectors again."

"They call themselves Protectors?" Max asked, shaking his head in disbelief.

"Villains always think they're the heroes," Rhodes said with a strained, sad smile. Then he turned to Wells, brightening. "What do you need from us next?"

"The basics," Wells said quickly. "Food, water, rest, medical help."

Rhodes nodded and reached out to shake Wells's hand. "Welcome back . . . Councilor Jaha."

CHAPTER 33

Clarke

"*Spiraea tomentosa*," Clarke's mother said softly, pressing a nondescript green leaf against the flat of her own hand. "That's my closest guess. A tea made from this one helps stomach upset, according to the book."

Mary leaned over to tap the old dusty tome that Max had given her during her recovery: a pre-Cataclysm book about local herbs. In the days that Clarke and the others had been gone, her parents had taken on a new initiative, bolstering the camp's dwindling supply of medicine by reproducing materials from the Colony and experimenting with local plants.

Clarke peered down at the leaf, memorizing each

detail, but it was her mother's hand that held her attention . . . warm, soft, alive. Dr. Lahiri said that her mother had healed up in record time.

"This one is called boneset," Clarke's mother went on, laying a plant with delicate white petals onto the table. "They used to think it helped set fractured bones, thus the name, but it was just superstition, unfortunately. It does, however, have some use in treating fevers, so I'm going to keep playing with it and see what we can develop . . ."

"You're amazing," Clarke said, hugging her mother gently, careful not to jostle her injury.

"'Amazing' . . ." Clarke's father walked in from the field, where he'd been helping dig foundations for new cabins. He dusted his hands off on his trousers with a grin. "That's high praise coming from a girl who just stormed a fortress."

"Hardly," Clarke said, flushing. "I didn't do it alone."

"But you did it," her mother said, her eyes shining. "We're proud of you."

Clarke felt proud too, looking around at the quickly rebuilding camp. Their people may have been damaged by the attack—but they hadn't been defeated. They'd healed up and set to work.

They'd all been so busy since returning yesterday. Clarke had immediately started helping out in the infirmary; a few of the people they'd brought with them from the Stone had needed more rigorous medical care. Glass had volunteered to oversee clearing and planting the Colonists' very first field. Wells was reinvigorated, helping out with the Council, and Luke's engineering mind been electrified by all the new plans.

And they weren't going to re-create what they'd had before . . . they had the courage to reimagine something even better. There were plans for a waterwheel in the nearby stream that could power devices in the camp, and a schoolhouse with a playground. This place wasn't just coming back to life; it was being reborn as something joyous, a real village that Clarke couldn't wait to be a member of.

"Clarke."

Bellamy's voice rose up from the doorway. Clarke turned to greet him—and her smile fell. His brow was furrowed, his shoulders tense. Something was wrong.

"Can we talk?" he asked quickly, glancing over one shoulder, his foot digging into the dirt. "It's important."

"Sure," she said, hurrying carefully past her few remaining patients. "Of course."

Bellamy's hand was cold against hers as he led her through the bustling camp. Octavia and Anna were leading the kids in a boisterous game of tag. In the center of camp, Glass and Luke looked over a sketch of perimeter watchtowers. Bellamy pulled Clarke past the ovens, where fresh bread was baking; past Wells, who was etching Graham's name into a grave marker; all the way out to the site where new cabin foundations were being dug.

Clarke's stomach clenched tighter with every step. What had Bellamy seen? Was there a new danger already? Or had he thought about it and decided that he wasn't ready to forgive her, after all?

They eventually reached a cleared patch of charred grass in the corner of the camp. Bellamy stopped and turned silently to face Clarke, his eyebrows raised as though he was waiting for some sort of a reaction.

She shook her head, glancing around, finding nothing particularly worrying here.

"What do you think?" he said, gesturing around him.

"Think of what?"

His eyes darted around nervously. "The view from this spot."

"Um . . . it's nice?"

"Good . . . good . . ." Then he took a deep breath and said, "Do you think it'd be a good spot for a cabin? For the two of us?"

Clarke's head grew fuzzy as she tried to make sense of his words. "A cabin for . . ."

Then, in an instant, Bellamy's nervousness seemed

to drain away. "For us, Clarke." He took her hand and squeezed it . . . and slowly got down on one knee.

"*Oh*," Clarke said, her voice no more than a breath.

He reached into his pocket and pulled out a silver ring.

"Bellamy," she whispered. "Where did you get that?"

"I traded for it," he said, almost as cavalier as usual . . . except for the fact that his hands were trembling.

Then she recognized it—the deep blue stone in the center—and her hands flew up to her chest, pressing hard to keep her heart from bursting out of her. "Bel, that's . . . that's . . ."

"A Griffin family heirloom," he said, grinning.

"Where did you . . . how did you . . . ?" She shook her head, speechless. This was the stone her ancestors had brought with them to the Colony from Earth, passed down through her family for generations.

"Like I said, I traded for it . . . with your mother." He held it out to her, tentatively, almost as if there was a part of him that didn't believe she'd take it.

But she did, cradling it in her palm. "What did you trade for it?"

"A promise," Bellamy said, reaching out to cup her hand in both of his. "I promised to love you, respect you, honor you, protect you, defend you, tease you, argue with you . . ." He laughed. "And so on and so on . . ." His face fell serious. "For the rest of my life and yours . . . Clarke, will you marry me?"

Her knees gave out. She put her hands on his shoulders and let herself slide to the ground beside him, her arms slung around his shoulders, her kiss serving as the only answer he would ever need.

But just in case, she drew away and murmured against his lips, "Yes."

They kissed again, and as they sat in the soil, entwined together, it felt to Clarke as if it wasn't just this tiny patch of land they were claiming, it was the whole camp, the hills and mountains and rivers and lakes around them and everything beyond that.

Despite everything they'd faced since landing on Earth, right now it seemed as though the entire planet was finally saying what Bellamy was murmuring to her right now.

"Welcome home."

ACKNOWLEDGMENTS

Working on this series has been the privilege of a lifetime, and I'm so very grateful to all the people who've helped turn my dream into a reality.

Thank you to everyone at Alloy for your support, encouragement, and creativity at every stage of this adventure. Special thanks to Sara Shandler, Josh Bank, Les Morgenstein, Lanie Davis, Theo Guliadis, Annie Stone, Liz Dresner, and Heather David. Extra special thanks to the brilliant Joelle Hobeika, whose unmatched imagination sparked the idea for *The 100*; the incomparable Romy Golan, who turns strings of words into gorgeous books and keeps us from descending into chaos; and the hugely talented Eliza Swift, who is a fount of editorial wisdom, and is an absolute joy to work with.

Huge thanks to everyone at Little, Brown and Hodder & Stoughton, including Pam Gruber, Leslie Shumate, Saraciea Fennell, Emily Kitchin, and Becca Mundy.

An extra round of space hugs to the fabulous team at the Rights People who are responsible for introducing this series to readers around the world. I'd also like to thank the incredible editors, translators, designers, and publishers who've created such gorgeous foreign editions of The 100 books. Connecting with your readers is the most incredible privilege. Thank you for helping me share my stories.

Thank you to the dazzlingly talented Jenn Marie Thorne, who helped bring this book to life in countless ways. You are a rock star, and I remain in awe of your amazing brain.

And, most of all, thank you to my readers. You've made me feel like the luckiest author in the world.